Bronwyn Parry's six romantic thrillers set in remote NSW combine the emotion of a contemporary romance with the tension of a fast-paced crime plot and have been published in Australia, the UK, Germany and the Czech Republic. Her novels have won or been shortlisted for numerous awards, including the Romance Writers of America's prestigious Golden Heart, RITA, and Daphne du Maurier awards, the Australian Romance Readers awards for Favourite Romantic Suspense, and her fifth novel, Storm Clouds, is the first romantic suspense novel to be shortlisted for the Davitt Awards for crime fiction by Australian women.

The North Wind, a Christmas novella, is a slight change of pace from Bronwyn's usual gritty romantic thriller. It's set in the same small town as the books in the Dungirri series, and there is a mystery to solve – but it's not quite as gritty and dangerous as the other books. It is Christmas, after all.

Bronwyn lives in the New England tablelands of northern NSW and loves to travel in Australia's wild places.

Also by Bronwyn Parry

The Dungirri Series:
As Darkness Falls
Dark Country
Darkening Skies

The Goodabri Series:
Dead Heat
Storm Clouds
Sunset Shadows

All published by Hachette Australia

Note: The books in each series are loosely-
linked, and can be read as stand alone books.

The North Wind

A Dungirri Christmas Novella

Bronwyn Parry

Firetail Press
Armidale NSW Australia

Published by Firetail Press, Armidale, NSW, Australia, 2016

978-0-9941970-2-3 (paperback)

Cover design by Lauren Sadow and Bronwyn Parry
Cover photo by Bronwyn Parry

Dedication

My Mum was my greatest supporter and knew and loved the people of Dungirri as if they were real. She wanted me to write all their stories. So this one's for you, Mum. I'm sorry it took so long, but you were with me as I wrote it, and you're with me, always.

CHAPTER 1

'Are you *sure* this is where you want to go, Granddad? This place is in the middle of nowhere.' Owen slowed the car to avoid a kangaroo hopping across the dirt road and glanced at his grandfather.

In the passenger seat, Bernard Chynoweth sat with his hands lightly clasped in his lap. He'd hardly spoken since they'd picked up the hire car at Dubbo Airport a couple of hours ago, but everything about his quietness was calm.

'I'm sure, Owen.'

When he'd promised to take his grandfather anywhere he wanted to go for the Christmas season, Owen had expected they'd be heading for London, or Vienna, or one of Bernard's other favourite cities in Europe to enjoy concerts, comfortable hotels and excellent food. Not driving on a sandy road into outback New South Wales to a tiny dot on the map he'd never heard of.

Dungirri did have a hotel, but the rate he'd been quoted when he phoned to book a twin room indicated it would be basic. That didn't worry him

– some of the places he'd worked he'd been lucky to have any sort of roof to sleep under – but it was a far cry from what he'd had in mind to mark his grandfather's ninetieth birthday. And Bernard still hadn't told him *why*. Why he'd insisted, in his courteous, determined way, that he wanted to go to Dungirri now, this year.

With failing health, Bernard couldn't have made the trip alone, and Owen didn't begrudge the time and effort at all, but this mystery from a man who'd always been open and honest? Puzzling. Worrying, so that he watched his grandfather closely for symptoms of dementia. Yet he saw only this calm, quiet determination.

A white utility pulled out of a side road a hundred metres in front of him, turning towards Dungirri, and Owen lifted his foot from the accelerator as the dust thrown up by the ute billowed towards him along the road and obscured his vision. Keeping well back, he followed the dust cloud over a low bridge and on to the sealed road of the town.

Not much of a town. An old timber community hall and a police station on the right after the bridge. Vacant blocks, a few houses, and a rural supplies store on the left.

The ute ahead of him was already parked in the driveway of a white weatherboard house and the driver, a young woman with the relaxed air of a local, raised her hand in a casual country wave at their oncoming car.

He caught a glimpse as he drove past of a shapely butt clad in faded jeans. Yes, he noticed it. Not that he'd ever be so crass as to comment about it. Thirty-something male with a healthy appreciation of women. Not a sleazebag. Intelligence and personality mattered far more to him than appearance.

Christmas decorations hung from rows of lights strung across the street in the central block of the main street, and along the row of shop buildings on each side. Not that many of those buildings had seen actual trade in them for a while; other than the rural supplies store and a small general shop, most were long empty, a few boarded-up.

He shifted down a gear before the two-storey hotel at the end of the block, and indicated to turn left into the side street.

'Can you keep going on this road for a few minutes?' Bernard asked. 'There's a place I'd like to see, a few kilometres along.'

Owen checked the rear vision mirror. Nothing behind him. 'I thought you'd not been here before.'

'I haven't. Sylvia at the library looked up the address on the computer for me.'

Great. The librarian knew more about his grandfather's quest than he did. Maybe if he'd been home in Australia more often . . . None of them were. Not his brother, pursuing his music career in New York. Nor his sister, undertaking neurosurgery research in California. Leaving Bernard reliant on the local library to help him with the technology to communicate with them all.

That had to change. Owen had to change. Time to settle back in Australia.

The town petered out after the pub. A recently

cleared block of land. A dilapidated showground, the not-very-grand stand leaning to one side, a pavilion with boarded-up windows. A couple more houses, before paddocks and a sign for Birraga, sixty kilometres away.

'Whose address is it?' Owen ventured to ask.

Bernard's silence lasted at least a kilometre. 'A person I knew once.' He cleared his throat. 'I will tell you, lad. But I need to find out some more information, first. The place should be a couple of kilometres further up, on the left. I'd be grateful if you could drive slowly past it.'

With no other traffic on the road, Owen dropped his speed. The dry forest to the east of Dungirri gave way here to flat brown paddocks, scattered farms, pockets of scrub. A few kilometres along, a steel machinery shed and a driveway over a grid indicated another farm. The house – if it belonged to the same place – was two hundred metres further on, an older-style white-painted homestead with a white picket and chook-wire fence enclosing a yard with a minimal garden.

Owen shifted down to second gear. Two people stood in the driveway, beside a small car. An older woman with her hand on the driver's door, neatly dressed in blue trousers and a light-coloured blouse. The other person in baggy checked shirt over loose jeans and a head of unruly grey hair, leaning on a shovel. Owen had to take a second glance. Not particularly feminine, but definitely female. Both women noticed the slow vehicle.

Bernard quickly turned his face away. 'Thank you.

We can go back to the hotel now.'

'*Which woman?*' Owen wanted to ask. Perhaps it wasn't the women, but the house that his grandfather had wished to see. Not that Owen could think of any reason why a property out here in the back of beyond could be of interest to Bernard. But he held his tongue and did a u-turn to drive back to the Dungirri pub.

~

Christmas in Dungirri. Angie Butler changed her jeans to cooler cargo shorts in her old bedroom in the family home and wished herself somewhere, anywhere else. She could have gone to Bali with friends. Or sailing on the Great Barrier Reef. Or hiking in Tasmania. But no, family duty called and here she was, back in her old home town. Back in her old home. The first Christmas since her father's sudden death. Maybe the last Christmas in this house, in Dungirri. If – a big if – her mother could sell the pub.

Her mother fussed in the kitchen, the kettle already on the boil. Tea. Oh, God, the first of how many gazillion cups of tea she'd have to drink over the next week. Nancy Butler didn't keep any decent coffee in the house. Or any alcohol. A publican's wife for thirty-five years, she hated the smell of both of them. She also refused to use teabags in her house. She only used leaf tea, brewed to death in the old brown teapot.

Sitting on the too-soft single bed, Angie eased her

feet out of her boot socks and steeled herself for her mother's onslaught. *Why don't you get a nice job in an office? You're thirty. When are you going to settle down? Don't swear. It's unladylike.*

A week. Just a week. And her mother meant well, even if her views of women's ideal lives were stuck somewhere in the nineteen-fifties. Along with the house décor. There'd never been spare money to update the third-generation Butler home.

Angie headed barefoot on the smooth polished floorboards to the kitchen.

Her mother had the old Bushells tea caddy in one hand and the teaspoon in the other, hovering over the teapot, her fingers shaking so that tiny black leaves fell. She gave a nervous laugh when she saw Angie. 'I can't remember how much I put in,' she said, and dumped the spoonful in the pot.

Great. Short-term memory problems. Her mother was only sixty.

'Don't look at me like that, Angela.' The tea caddy banged back on its shelf. 'I'm not losing my marbles. I'm just . . .' She suddenly sank down into a chair. 'He's made an offer for the pub. Gillespie has. The agent called an hour ago. I don't know what to do.'

Sell. Angie bit her tongue. 'Is it a good offer?'

Her lips pursed, Nancy gave a grudging nod, and named a figure under the asking price but within the realm of what they expected.

Angie weighed her words carefully while she took over making the tea and poured the boiling water into the teapot. 'It's been on the market for eight months. You haven't had any other offers in that time, have you?' Rhetorical question, really. But she wanted to help her mother work through the situation logically.

'No.'

Instead of reaching for a homely mug, Angie carried one of her grandmother's blue floral teacups and saucers from the dresser and placed it in front of her mother. She kept her voice gentle. Persuasion, not argument. No sense backing Nancy into a corner. 'You know you're not likely to get any more than that, Mum. Not here in Dungirri.'

'I know. But . . . it's *Gillespie*.'

'He is a local, Mum. He knows this place.'

'He's been away for *years*. In *prison*.'

Two cardinal sins in her mother's very proper view of the world: leaving Dungirri, and being a criminal.

Angie sat at the table with another of Grandma's tea cups, half terrified she'd break the fine china. That would be another cardinal sin. 'He was innocent, Mum. His conviction was quashed years ago. And now he's come back again and chosen to stay. Without him and Deb and Liam these past few months the pub would have gone broke and shut up.'

Three months, she'd worked in the pub with her brother after their father's sudden death, trying to keep it running. They'd had to take leave from their jobs to return to Dungirri, keep paying rent on accommodation elsewhere, and work long hours trying to sort out their father's affairs and get the pub ready for sale – a huge strain for both of them. The fortuitous arrival of Gil Gillespie in town with his two friends had eased the situation, given their experience running a pub in Sydney, and Deb's and Liam's need for work while Gil dealt with other issues. They'd not only kept the pub open, but given it more life – and income – than it had seen in years.

Nancy gave a disdainful sniff, unwilling to concede any point. 'His father was a drunkard. And a wife-beater.'

And a whole lot worse, if even half the stories Angie had heard were true. 'Gil is neither, Mum.'

Another sniff.

'Mum, you don't have to make a decision right away. Think about the options. You can hang out for a better offer, but they're not exactly queuing up, are they? Or perhaps you could make a counter offer to Gil. Or you could ask him his plans for the place.'

Her mother started as though she'd suggested something outrageous. 'Oh, I couldn't do that. Not talk to him.' She took refuge in a sip of tea, and Angie's heart ached for her, for the narrow life and experiences and her lack of confidence and trust in people with different life experiences. With her tea cup still clasped in her hands Nancy looked over it to her daughter. 'But you could. You can ask them. You can find out, can't you? I wouldn't want, you know, for him to put in gaming machines or betting.'

Angie doubted that gambling of any form featured in Gil's plans for the hotel. But she'd have to check before assuring her mother of that point. It might tip the scales in Gil's favour, and the sooner the pub was sold, the better for everybody.

As long as it sold to the right buyer. Dungirri sure as hell didn't need some investor to buy the pub who didn't give a fig about the town and installed poker machines and betting facilities to up the turnover – facilities that would send too many vulnerable people in the struggling town broke, and only line the owner's pockets.

'I'll go up there in a little while, and see what I can find out,' she promised her mother. Less than half an hour at home, and already she was grateful for an excuse to escape.

~

Bernard opted to lie down for a rest after they'd checked into the pub and Owen helped him up the flight of stairs to their room. A simple room, but clean and functional, with twin beds, a wardrobe, a small table, and a comfortable arm chair. French doors opened out on to the wide, shady veranda, overlooking the main street. Despite the summer heat, an overhead fan created a cooling breeze.

By the time Owen brought their bags up from the car and returned to the hotel room, his grandfather was asleep on one of the twin beds, breathing easily, his limbs relaxed. But now that he had the opportunity to watch him unobserved, Owen couldn't ignore the changes in the past year: the paper-thin skin stretched tighter over the fine bones of his face and his hands and the increasing frailty of the man who'd been an inspiration and one of the pillars in his life.

Bernard would turn ninety the day after Christmas. Owen didn't expect his grandfather to see many more birthdays after that. Just as well he'd come home to Australia. It would be up to him to care for Bernard in these last years. Up to him to support his grandfather in whatever this mystery involved.

He left Bernard sleeping and went downstairs to see what he could find out about Dungirri.

The young Asian-Australian barman who'd given him the room key had few customers to serve. Not surprising, for mid-afternoon on a weekday. He carried a mug of coffee out to the courtyard, to a man working at a laptop at a table in the shade of a tree. The thought of coffee tempted Owen – he'd only had airport coffee today – but he needed exercise and to stretch muscles more than he needed a caffeine hit. Given Dungirri's small size, it wouldn't take long to walk around it.

Despite all the empty store buildings, there were signs of a good community spirit. In addition to the Christmas decorations hung along the verandas, one of the empty shops featured a window display of a life-sized stuffed Santa in a red singlet and shorts, reclining in a rocking chair, with stuffed toys of various Australian animals at his feet. A mural covered the next window, a more traditional nativity scene, although instead of sheep and donkeys, a possum, kangaroos and a koala gazed at the baby doll in the cradle.

A small poster on the side of the building advertised a guitar for sale. A classical guitar. Not professional level – nothing like his brother would play – but not an el-cheapo model, either, with a solid cedar top, rosewood back and sides and an ebony fingerboard. *'Well looked after,'* the sign read. *'But I never play it.'*

Owen missed his guitar, lying now in cinders beneath the ruins of a Kabul hotel.

He didn't need a new guitar.

He dragged his gaze away from the phone number. Another poster immediately below the guitar one advertised Carols by Candlelight in the Memorial Hall. Presumably the hall up in the next block that they'd passed on the way in. Tonight. Seven-thirty. Maybe he'd see if his grandfather wanted to go.

A sharp sound, like a gunshot, startled him and he tensed, ready to duck, but it was only the thwack of a screen door falling shut at the house next to the shop. The woman who'd driven into town ahead of them walked down the drive to the street. She'd changed into cargo shorts and she walked with an easy stride, the breeze playing with her hair.

She grinned as she approached. An open, friendly smile that said she was perfectly at ease here, in this town. That relaxed confidence threw him for a moment. The places he'd been, most of the past few years, a woman – especially a lone woman – would never go anywhere near an unknown male. They would cross to the other side of the street, or turn around, or go into a shop or house.

'Hi,' she said, and stopped to look at the posters. 'First time we've had Carols by Candlelight in years.'

She gave him a quick sideways glance, but he knew that because she caught him looking at her. Tawny brown hair pulled back into a casual pony-tail, blue-grey eyes with a playful light in an oval face without makeup. Not classically pretty, but he found the lively energy . . . yeah, *attractive*. Maybe because this was a peaceful little town in rural Australia and she wasn't on edge, afraid of being blown up or bombed or gunned down or kidnapped.

He had to get his head back from there to *here*. Peaceful country town. Australia. Christmas. His grandfather.

'Will it be okay for visitors to go?' he asked. 'We're just in town for a few days. My grandfather and I. We wouldn't want to intrude.'

'I knew you weren't a local. But don't worry, it's a fundraiser for the local school kids, so the more the merrier. Bring your wallets for a good cause. You're visiting someone here?'

She probably knew everyone in town. He searched for a way to explain why they were here, and didn't find one. Because he had no clue why they were here. 'I'm travelling with my grandfather,' he said. 'He likes to see new places.' That was truthful.

Her eyebrows rose. 'And you chose Christmas in Dungirri?'

'He did. I'm just the chauffeur.'

'That's dedication.'

'I've been away a lot. It's good to have some time with him. Besides, this place is peaceful and there are no Christmas shopping crowds.' No-one out on the street except the two of them. No terrorist bombers targeting excited families preparing for a celebration. And there he was, with his head back in Baghdad again.

But she definitely wasn't in Baghdad. Not with

her hands casually in her pockets and her unhurried, small-town friendliness. 'No Christmas shopping, full stop. You'll have to go in to Birraga if you want to buy anything other than milk or,' she nodded at the Rural Supplies store just along the street, 'fencing wire.'

After all the months overseas, of hard desperate work and constant tension, he found himself reluctant to break off this light, pleasant conversation. 'Not something I've ever had much need for,' he said. 'I confess I'm tempted by the guitar, though. Do you know the guy selling it?'

She read the sign quickly. 'That will be Ryan Wilson. Good bloke. Had a rugby accident a few years back and injured his spine. I didn't know he played the guitar, though. But you do?'

'Yeah, sometimes.'

An old utility drove down the road past them and swung in to park in front of the rural store. The woman he was speaking with raised her hand in a country wave, but it took Owen several seconds until the driver clambered out of the ute to recognise, under the battered felt hat, one of the older women from the house his grandfather had been interested in.

The driver spared them an unsmiling nod before she strode in to the store. That brief, brief interaction left Owen with the disconcerting sense that he should know her. Yet he couldn't place her in his fairly-good memory for faces.

'Is she someone famous?' he asked his new acquaintance.

'Delphi?' She laughed lightly. 'Nope. Not unless she has a secret life none of us know about. She has a property a few k's out of town.'

Curiosity about his grandfather's mystery and the temptation to keep the conversation going made him probe lightly, 'Her name is Delphi? That's unusual.' And the mythic nature of the name seemed something of a disconnect with the very down-to-earth appearance of the woman.

'Philadelphia O'Connell. Her family has been in the district since the 1870s. But there's only her and her niece left now. Two of her uncles died in the war. Her brother was the author, Patrick O'Connell.' She laughed self-consciously but enthusiasm still lit her eyes. 'Sorry. You didn't ask for their family history. I did an assignment on the O'Connells as early settlers when I was in high school. Delphi showed me her grandfather's journals.'

The O'Connell family had been here for generations. But his grandfather had only come from England to Queensland in the 1940s. Owen couldn't see how there could be a connection.

'Have your family been here as long?' he asked.

'No.' She nodded towards the house she'd come from. 'My great-grandfather bought that house and the pub in the 1940s. But I don't live in Dungirri now.'

Where do you live? He swallowed back the question that might have been interpreted as a clumsy pick-up line. 'Does your family still own the pub?' he asked instead.

'My mum does. But hopefully not for long.

Speaking of which, I'm on a mission to make sure it sells. I'll see you around, I'm sure.'

As she ambled off he pretended to look at the posters again so that he could watch her out of the corner of his eye. But after only a few steps she swivelled around, walking backwards as she asked with an irreverent grin, 'Can you sing?'

He answered her question with the simple truth. 'Yes.' The advantage of a musical family. He could hold a tune well.

'Good. Come to the Carols. The supper will be worth it, I promise.' She raised her hand in a farewell gesture and continued on her way without looking back.

He strolled down the road towards the creek. Had she been flirting? Had he been flirting? He didn't think so, but he definitely felt a spark of . . . something. Attraction. Interest. Enjoyment. Possibly mutual. Probably mutual. Not that it meant anything. Perfectly natural for a single, heterosexual thirty-four-year-old male to notice with pleasure an attractive, upbeat woman. Especially when there was little more to worry about. No bombs, no soldiers, no terrorists, no fighting.

Christmas in Dungirri might be more enjoyable than he'd anticipated.

~

The front bar was empty, but Angie resisted the temptation to sneak a look at the guest registration book to find out the visiting guy's name. Just because she could easily have looked didn't mean she should. Her mother might own the hotel but Angie no longer worked there, and despite her curiosity she did respect the privacy of the guests.

She'd see him again, she'd introduce herself, and then she'd find out his name. A stranger in Dungirri was a rarity. A stranger with eyes that reminded her of storm clouds and sunshine, sparkling against shadows. Not a shallow man, whoever he was. And good-looking. Faded jeans, a white cotton shirt, no wedding ring, not much use for fencing wire, but he played the guitar. Interesting. Especially in a town with a shortage of single, interesting men around her age.

But the stranger would have to remain a mystery for the moment, until after she'd seen another interesting, probably not unattached man. Although "interesting" wasn't the right word for *him*. Complex. Complicated. And, if rumour had it right, committed to Kris Matthews, the local police sergeant. Maybe that's why he'd offered to buy the pub.

Angie helped herself to a glass of water and went out to talk with him.

Gil Gillespie sat in the shade of the towering old kurrajong tree, staring at his laptop. She didn't know him well. She'd been a kid still in primary school when they'd arrested and jailed him on a trumped up charge, eighteen years ago. And when he returned in September there'd only been a couple of days before he'd disappeared again, into hiding. But his friends Liam and Deb had stayed, and she knew them better. Not an easy man, Gil, but their fierce loyalty to him spoke volumes about the man he'd become.

At eleven years old she wouldn't have dared speak to the tough, silent teenager in case some of the darker rumours were true. She wasn't eleven anymore, she'd learned the truth behind the rumours, and he'd risked his life more than once to protect people he cared about. But a hint of nervousness surfaced anyway, and instead of a calm greeting and reasoned statement, she opened with, 'You've got my mother all in a tizzy.'

He spared her a glance. Given his habitual reticence, that constituted an almost warm welcome. 'No business of mine if she can't make a simple decision, objectively.'

She sat opposite him at the sturdy wooden table. 'But it's not that simple. And you know it.'

He merely shrugged. 'She distrusts me. Good luck to her selling the place to anyone else.' He returned his attention to his laptop, scribbling a few figures on a writing pad beside it.

Angie couldn't risk leaving it at that. He'd sold a pub in Sydney, had plenty of money, and he sure as hell didn't need this deal to go through. But Dungirri needed him. 'Look, my mum always hated the pub, and the demands it made on our family. But she cares about this community. She wants to know your plans for the place before she decides.'

'Is she worried that I'm going to set the hotel up as a half-way house for unreformed murderers?'

Maybe it said something about her mother's gradually softening attitude to Gil that she hadn't expressed something like that as a concern. 'Don't put the fear in her head. She wants to know if you intend to introduce gaming machines.'

'Why would I do that?'

'I kept the books for several months. I know how bad the figures are. Gaming machines might increase the income.'

'You weren't serving meals. There was no web presence, no way for tourists to find and book accommodation. And you were being ripped off by suppliers.'

The blunt truths smarted. Her dad hadn't exactly embraced the twenty-first century, and almost everything about the hotel had remained in his comfort zone – circa 1980. She took a sip of her water, the glass cool against her fingers. 'Mum fell apart when Dad died. Despite their different personalities they were close. Dave and I came back and did our best but . . . It was a difficult time, sorting out Dad's affairs for Mum. We barely kept our heads above water. You don't know how grateful I am to Deb and Liam for stepping in. We couldn't have coped, couldn't have kept the hotel open without them.'

'Yeah. I've seen the figures.' He spoke so drily it made her thirsty.

'And you still made an offer to buy?'

He opened a document on the laptop and swivelled the screen around so that she could see it. A spreadsheet, with three columns: bar receipts, meals, accommodation. Week by week, the income figures edged upwards. All due to Liam and Deb, who'd worked for Gil in Sydney for years, Liam as barman, Deb as a darned fine cook. Best thing her mother had done, agreeing to employ them when Gil disappeared into witness protection.

'You think you can make it work?' she asked Gil. 'Make the pub a success?'

He closed the laptop, picked up his mug and rose to his feet. 'Success is a relative term. But I wouldn't have made the offer if I didn't think it could be made viable.'

She'd heard that he had transformed a run-down suburban pub in Sydney into a thriving business. 'Dungirri needs your skills and experience, Gil. This town will die if the pub closes.'

'I'm no frigging saviour. And don't go thinking that money will be enough. If Dungirri's going to survive, it needs more than a pub. It needs people to stay here, and work and raise families.'

She couldn't tell, from his expressionless face, if that was a general observation or a criticism aimed at her, for leaving the town. 'The only employment in the district is casual, or short-term contract, and there's very little of that. Most of it has been with the Flanagans.' And since she didn't do corruption or extortion, or have any wish to sleep with any of the Flanagan men to get a job, she'd left town.

'The Flanagans are gone,' Gil said flatly, with no triumph or pleasure in the words, as if he'd had nothing to do with exposing the family and their mafia connections. But he'd paid a high price for his actions, with his daughter and friends injured in addition to the critical injuries that had almost taken his own life.

'They are,' she acknowledged. 'But I'm not expecting major investment or increased opportunities to come flooding in. Not out here. Employment might be worse than ever.' She caught her error too late. She shouldn't have been negative about the outlook for the district. Not to the man who had offered to buy the business. 'Although maybe,' she added hastily, 'investment in the town will encourage more investment.'

He only snorted, as if he'd read right through her, and turned away.

'You didn't answer my question,' she said to his retreating back. 'About gaming machines.'

He barely paused. 'No machines. No betting. I don't take money from vulnerable people.' The screen door slammed behind him as he went inside.

She finished her water slowly, out here under the Kurrajong tree where she'd played as a child, keeping out of the way of her parents working inside. The pub had been their life, their world, dictating their family activities from sunrise to late at night, seven days a week. No days off, no holidays. She'd never been further than Birraga until a High School trip to Dubbo when she was thirteen, after which she'd joined sports teams, trained hard, so that she could travel to other towns and cities to compete at regional and state titles. At eighteen she'd escaped to university in Canberra and stayed away except for the obligatory visits home for Christmas most years – when she'd usually ended up spending most of her time in the pub, pulling beers, cooking meals, washing sheets, and giving her mother a short break from the constant round of work, work, work.

They had to sell, and soon. Without the hotel Nancy would finally be free to enjoy life without the weight of the struggling business on her shoulders.

But despite the truth of Gil's words – that Dungirri wouldn't survive without people staying – Angie couldn't see a place for herself in the district. She had a job, a good career, which took her travelling all over the country. After Christmas she'd leave again. If, once the pub sold, her mother decided to move east to be closer to her sisters, Angie might never return to Dungirri.

CHAPTER 2

Even after the exercise of his walk, jet lag dragged at Owen. With his grandfather still sleeping when he returned to their room, he took the opportunity to lie down himself, just for a short while.

He woke with a start from a deep sleep. A bad dream slipped from his mind without leaving any details but the uneasiness of it remained in him, a tightness at the back of his neck, his fists clenched, and it took effort to refocus on here and now. At least he hadn't muttered or called out in his dream, because his grandfather sat at the small table, writing in a journal, unaware he had woken.

His watch read almost six o'clock. Two hours, he'd been asleep. Hell. He swung around to sit on the edge of the bed, massaging the lingering tension from his neck. 'It's been a while since I napped longer than you, Granddad. You should have woken me.'

Fountain pen poised on the page, Bernard gave him a quick study with paternal – and doctorly – concern. 'You were tired. You've been pushing yourself too hard for too long. There was no need to wake you yet.'

Great. Now his ninety-year old grandfather was looking after *him*, instead of the other way around. 'I'm fine.' Mostly. He'd be over the jetlag and fatigue in a day or two. Probably. It always took a few days to adjust back to Australian life. 'Hey, I found out they're having carols by candlelight in town tonight, starting at seven-thirty. I thought you might like to go. But we should get some dinner first.'

Bernard agreed on dinner, demurred his decision on the carols. 'Give me a few minutes to finish this.' With a wry smile, he added, 'Before I forget what I'm writing.'

Owen noted the comment but hadn't seen much evidence of memory problems. 'Are you starting your memoir at last?' he probed. It couldn't count as nagging if he only asked every six months.

'Not yet, lad. No, this is just some memories.' He returned to his writing without any further explanation, so Owen went in search of the bathroom at the end of the veranda – its décor still somewhere in the 1960s – and splashed his face with cold water to jolt his brain cells fully awake.

When he returned, his grandfather was placing the journal in the vintage leather briefcase he'd brought as carry-on on the plane, and Owen caught only a glimpse of a number of albums or journals before he closed it up again. No answers to the mystery for now, then.

His grandfather leant heavily on his arm as they carefully descended the once-grand staircase, and as they contemplated the dinner menu at the bar, he seemed distracted, his thoughts drifting elsewhere. Owen had to prompt him to choose what he wanted for dinner. Waving off Bernard's apology for his absent-mindedness, Owen picked up their drinks and suggested that they sit out in the courtyard, away from the noise of the small crowd in the front bar.

The sun still shone hot, but low in the sky, making the courtyard shaded and pleasant. Out here only a few tables were occupied. A group of four men and women in their twenties talked and laughed at a table in the corner, relaxed and easy together. A family with three girls, the youngest a pre-schooler, shared a pizza at another table. The mother had her arm in a cast and the father used a wheelchair, with the strong upper body of a man who'd been confined to one for some time. Ryan Wilson, perhaps. But despite the injuries their happiness and the obvious affection and love between the couple and their kids reminded Owen of his own parents, both strong and loving through their illnesses. A bitter-sweet mix of nostalgia and grief for them caught him unawares, stronger than usual. Probably because his grandfather's health issues and increasing frailty couldn't be ignored. The failing aortic heart valve meant Owen would lose him, too.

All the more reason to make this time with him count, and to support him in whatever time he had left. While they waited for their meals, Owen sought for a way to raise the topic of Philadelphia O'Connell. Of the two women they'd seen at the house, his instinct said that it was her that Bernard had known.

Moisture from condensation trickled down the side of his glass and he took a mouthful of the cold cider to wet his dry throat. 'You said this afternoon that you needed to find some more information for your quest. Is that something that I can help you with? I can make discreet inquiries, if you like.'

Bernard sat back in his chair, his glass in his hands, and thought for some moments before he answered. 'Thank you, Owen. I haven't decided, yet, exactly what I will do. But I will ask for your help if I need it.'

The screen door of the pub opened with a squeak and the woman he'd spoken with earlier came through, carrying two baskets of bread. She left one with the group at the corner table, then brought the other across to where Owen and his grandfather sat.

The aroma of fresh crusty bread wafted as she placed the basket on their table. She smiled courteously at Bernard but her eyes danced with light as she grinned at Owen. 'Compliments of the management. Welcome to Dungirri.'

He couldn't help but grin in response. No mistaking the playful, light-hearted flirting. Or the probability that she'd used the bread as an excuse to say hello. Yet there was astuteness in her eyes, an intelligent appraisal of far more than his appearance. He wasn't sure what she'd see. He stood, holding out his hand. 'Thank you to the management. I'm Owen Caldwell.'

She shook his hand with firm assurance, her palm warm against his. 'Angela Butler. Angie, to everyone but my Mum.'

'This is my grandfather, Bernard Chynoweth.'

'Oh, please don't get up, Mr Chynoweth,' Angie protested as Bernard tried to rise. 'It's a pleasure to meet you both.'

The basics covered, conversation stalled for a moment and Owen searched for something else to say, something to keep her there for a little longer. 'I didn't realise you'd be working here.'

'I'm not really. Just co-opted to waitress for an hour. Jeanie's helping out at the hall so Deb's short-staffed in the kitchen. But don't panic,' she joked, 'I'm not cooking.' She paused for a breath then asked in something of a rush, 'Will we be seeing you at the Carols tonight?'

He looked over to his grandfather. 'Granddad?'

Bernard considered it for only a moment. 'Best if I don't go,' he said quietly. 'But you go, Owen. I'll have an early night.'

Very unlike his grandfather to turn down a community Christmas event involving music. He'd been a stalwart of his town orchestra for decades. *Best if I don't go* . . . 'What did that mean? Was he not feeling well? Or was his reluctance related to his mystery? Not questions Owen could ask in front of Angie.

'I'll probably come down for a while,' he told her.

'It won't be a late night,' she said. 'But it's for a good cause. The Dungirri school bus was in a bad crash a few weeks ago. Some of the kids and the two teachers had to be airlifted to Tamworth and Sydney. So, it's to help them, and also to fund some other support services. Some of the kids were pretty shaken up, especially with both teachers badly hurt.'

A school bus crash, serious injuries . . . Owen tried not to imagine the scene, and the probable aftermath. He already had too many scenes like it in his memory. Whether it was Baghdad, Dungirri, or anywhere else, a major incident involving children created wave after wave of trauma. He swallowed. 'The whole town must be pretty shaken up.'

She nodded, her face grave. 'Yes. Especially after the last few years. This town's had a rough trot. But everyone's pulling together now.' She glanced back at the pub. 'I'd better keep moving. Your meals won't be long.'

Bernard drew out his wallet after she'd gone, and handed a hundred dollar note across the table. 'For the children's fund,' he said.

Owen nodded, tucking the note in his pocket. He'd add his own contribution later. They both knew the kinds of issues and complications that might arise for the children and their families, and for the town. Yet he found himself reluctant to discuss it, even with his grandfather. They'd only be here for a few days. He felt for them, but had no role here. Not his town, not his responsibility, not his place. He'd learned the hard lesson long ago that he couldn't do everything, save everyone, heal everyone.

As they buttered slices of the warm, crusty sourdough, he steered the conversation back to the problem where he might have some agency. 'When I was talking with Angie this afternoon,' he ventured, 'one of the women we saw at the farm went into a nearby shop.'

His grandfather stopped buttering, his knife hovering over the bread. Owen continued, watching him closely, 'Angie knows her. Her name is Philadelphia O'Connell. Her family has been here for generations. But the only ones left are her and her niece.' Which implied she had no husband, and no children. 'I don't know if that helps you.'

Bernard laid down his knife and placed it carefully on the edge of the plate, his hand showing small tremors as he let it go. 'It is helpful to know,' he acknowledged, without lifting his gaze.

Owen stayed silent, giving him space to say more if he wished to.

'I met her a long time ago,' Bernard said eventually. 'She may not remember me. She may not know the wrong I did her. But if she does-' He cleared his throat. 'It would not be right to surprise her in public.'

The mystery deepened. His steadfast, honourable grandfather doing wrong by a woman? Owen couldn't imagine it. But he focused only on the immediate for now. 'Is that why you don't want to go to the carols? In case she's there?'

'Yes.'

'Would you like me to contact her tomorrow? Ask if you can meet with her?'

Another short silence. 'Let me think on that some more.'

The screen door squeaked again but it was a younger woman, a teenager in a kitchen uniform who brought their meals while Angie delivered plates with towering burgers to the group at the other table.

Owen's steak took up half his plate, the rest filled with sautéed potatoes and vegetables. Enough to feed a family, in some of the places he'd been.

Bernard picked up his fork, poked at the lettuce in his salad, and changed the subject. 'What are your plans, after Christmas? Will you take another overseas assignment?'

Now it was Owen who had no ready answer. This morning's email remained unanswered. The one asking him if he could take an urgent assignment from mid-January. In Syria.

But his grandfather picked at his food with unsteady hands and Owen made his decision there and then. 'No. I'll stay in Australia for a while. I'll sign up for some locum work to start with. There's no shortage of that.'

'You could join a practice,' his grandfather observed. 'Or establish your own.'

'I could.' There were plenty of doors that would be open to him, especially in Brisbane. He'd have to make some decisions about what he wanted to do, longer term.

But that would have to wait until after Christmas. Until after he'd helped his grandfather resolve this quest that had brought him to Dungirri.

~

Angie strolled back to her mother's after her hour of helping out. She hadn't mentioned Gillespie's offer to buy the pub to anyone. If Liam, Deb, or Gil's teenage daughter Megan knew about it they kept quiet and made no attempt to influence her. Maybe they understood that the decision was her mother's, not hers. But working with Deb and Liam again, even for just a short time, and seeing their professionalism and the improvements they'd made gave her even more reasons to use to persuade her mother to accept the offer.

Despite their youth – both younger than her – they knew more about running a twenty-first century hotel than she did. And they enjoyed it far more than she ever had. She'd hated the nightmare months of being cooped up in the pub, managing the bar with her brother, battling the shoeboxes of paperwork in the claustrophobic office, and heating pies and sausage rolls as the only food on offer, because taking on cooking and kitchen management had been beyond her.

Now the kitchen sparkled, the menu gave new life to rural pub basics, the accounts were tidily filed and up to date, and accommodation bookings were coming in from the online listings.

Like Owen Caldwell and his grandfather.

Why on earth would an elderly gentleman and his grandson come to Dungirri, of all places, for Christmas? Neither of them seemed stark raving mad. Mr Chynoweth was old and frail and that sometimes brought confusion, but Owen . . . her impression of him, beyond the prime sample of eye candy, was of a serious, smart, and very sane man. Oh, he'd enjoyed her teasing but neither of them were taking *that* seriously. She knew nothing about him. He knew next to nothing about her. They were both only here for a few days, and then back to their lives elsewhere.

She pushed open the front door of the old family house and braced herself for whatever questions and complaints her mother had come up with in the last hour but silence greeted her. A note in the kitchen said she'd already headed over to the hall, and asked Angie to carry over the plastic cake boxes on the table.

Angie eased the lid off the first box. A perfect, icing-sugar-sprinkled sponge cake, layered with cream and strawberries. Good. Her mother's cooking enthusiasm, faded after her husband's death, must have been revived. Trust Nancy to rise to the community occasion and make more cakes for the supper than she could carry herself.

In her bedroom, Angie changed quickly out of her cargo shorts and t-shirt into a sleeveless summer dress. Heels and makeup? She shook her head at herself in the mirror. A dress - even a simple cotton one - verged close to too formal for Dungirri. Flat sandals, some moisturiser on her face, and a pendant necklace were as dressy as she'd go.

And yes, that was more care than she usually took with her appearance. But after the nightmares Dungirri had experienced and her own struggles of the past couple of years, she kept thinking of this carol service as a celebration. Survival. Community. Hope.

If Gillespie bought the pub, the town might even

have a future.

If, if, if.

Nancy's sponge cakes were so light that even two of them in cake boxes weighed little. However, carrying the high boxes together was awkward, and Angie held them carefully, determined not to jostle them and damage the fragile concoctions of sponge and cream and fruit. She set them down on a veranda chair to lock the front door, and paused again at the end of the driveway, resting them on the gatepost to adjust her grip.

That hundred metres down Bridge Road to the Memorial Hall had never seemed quite so long. If she dropped the cakes her mother might never speak to her again.

'Can I help you with those?'

Owen Caldwell's voice. She'd been so focused on the cakes she hadn't seen him approaching up the road. Impeccable timing.

'Please. They're not heavy but I'm sure this top one is going to slip, and that would be a disaster of epic proportions.'

He carefully removed the top box, long fingers gripping the base. 'This is supper?'

A kilo less weight from her arms, and a tonne from her nerves. Except for the stunning-man-in-close-proximity nerves. They kept jangling. 'This is a tiny part of supper. But you may have to fight your way through a scrum to get any. Mum's cakes and pies are popular. She never made her special cakes for the pub, only for community events and family birthdays.' Sheesh. She'd just prattled. She never prattled.

People were already arriving at the hall, some on foot, some parking their cars in the vacant block beside the police station. Dozens of pairs of eyes saw her walk up the road, side-by-side with Owen. She'd be fielding questions and dispelling rumours half the night.

The mid-summer sun had yet to set, but the low angle of the light edged the freshly-painted white walls of the old Memorial Hall with a touch of gold. In the recently mown paddock between the hall and the creek the Progress Association had set up a stage. Families spread rugs on the grass in front of it, and a group of young guys unloaded chairs from a truck to form a semi-circle around the edges.

'We'll take the cakes inside, first,' Angie told Owen. 'They'll serve supper from the kitchen.'

Into the lioness's den. Not only her mother but at least half of Nancy's friends would see her walk in with Owen, prompting their curiosity. And their imaginations. Mind you, if she let her own imagination run loose . . . nope, a waste of time going there.

Inside the hall, several women were laying out food on long tables set down the middle of the room. There'd be enough food – cakes, slices, savouries – to feed Dungirri for days. Probably half of Birraga, too.

Her mother, unpacking one of her lemon meringue pies, caught sight of Angie. 'You've arrived. Good. That can go here.' She glanced past Angie to Owen and her mouth fell open.

Angie pre-empted questions and assumptions with a quick and breezy introduction. 'This is Owen. He's staying at the pub and offered to help carry the cakes. Owen, this is Nancy, my mother.' She took the cake box from his hands. 'Thanks so much for your help. I hope you enjoy the carols.' She softened the dismissal with a smile and a silent plea for understanding.

He gave a quick nod to her and to her mother. 'Nice to meet you, Nancy. I hope to taste a piece of that pie later.' Turning to leave, he said to Angie, 'I hope I'll see you out there.'

To avoid the gleam in her mother's eye, she busied herself finding a place on the table for the cakes. But she did take one more sidelong peek at Owen as he headed to the door.

Jeanie Menotti carried a large urn out of the kitchen and Owen paused to let her pass in front of him. Jeanie thanked him – and almost stopped in her tracks.

That made two older women whose jaws had dropped on seeing him. Yes, the guy was striking, in a square jawed, rugged kind of way. Still, Angie hadn't thought he'd appeal to women thirty or more years his senior. Or rather, she hadn't ever imagined her mother, or Nancy's friend Jeanie, both widows, taking an interest in any male. And hell, that was pretty damned ageist of her. Her mother was barely sixty, despite the lines of hard work worn into her face that made her look older. And although Jeanie must be in her seventies, she had more energy and did more than some people half her age.

Ten or more women, most of them in their fifties or older, hurried around the hall, making everything ready. Angie dithered for a moment, undecided whether to go outside and catch up with friends her own age, introduce Owen around, or stay to help.

Jeanie was already lugging the second, larger urn from the kitchen, too big and heavy for her. Angie stayed. She took the urn from Jeanie, carried it to the coffee and tea table beside the smaller urn, and carted buckets of water to fill them.

Outside, a male voice tested the microphone, and then Frank William's voice encouraged everyone to gather around, find a place to sit, but not to light their candles yet.

'Angie, can you give me a hand with this?' her mother called, disappearing behind the drawn curtains on the stage.

Hidden from view for now, the decorated Christmas tree, a native cypress, stood taller than Angie. Fairy lights laced through its branches, switched off for now. Nancy hastily unpacked boxes of brightly wrapped gifts, each with a nametag, and Angie helped her arrange them around the base of the tree.

'Every child is getting two gifts,' Nancy explained. 'After the accident, they need some brightness, a happy Christmas. But money's pretty tight for most of the families, so Jeanie asked a publisher for some books, and a big toy shop for some toys, and we've made sure that there's something for each of the children, even the little ones and the high school children who weren't on the bus.'

Angie nodded agreement. Because the accident impacted on the other kids, too. Siblings hurt, scared, shocked; parents distracted; cousins and grandparents and neighbours all affected. And the high school kids travelled sixty kilometres each way on the bus to and from Birraga High School every day. She'd had a nightmare herself, imagining the high school bus crashing with her on it, the night she'd heard about the accident. It had to be a hundred times worse for the kids who lived in Dungirri now.

Nancy placed the last gift, and stood back to study the tree. 'Do you think it will do?'

Angie linked her arm through her mother's. 'Of course it will. It's beautiful. And when the lights go on, it will be magical. You've done a great job, Mum.'

'Oh, Jeanie helped. And Delphi. She cut the tree and brought it in. Most of the other ladies, they've been looking after their grandchildren, but we've had the time. I wanted to do something useful, you know?'

For once, Angie didn't read her mother's glance as critical, but rather as a woman feeling her way, under confident. So much had changed for her, these past few months.

Angie squeezed Nancy's arm to her. 'You've always done useful things, Mum. You've always helped others.' Outside, the band struck up a cheerful rendition of 'Jingle Bells', and the crowd burst in to song. '*Dashing through the snow...*'

The contrast to Dungirri in mid-summer, with the air still hot and dry, made Angie smile. Most of the Dungirri kids had probably never seen snow. But it didn't matter. Christmas, she'd learned, was what you made it. Peace, love and joy had to come from her own heart. A lot easier said than done, sometimes, but she wasn't a kid anymore.

'Come on, Mum,' she said. 'Let's go sing some carols together.'

~

Owen lifted the last stack of chairs off the back of a truck as the first song started. Offering to help out had been better than standing around alone, knowing no-one other than Angie.

'We should have hired more chairs from Birraga,' Karl Sauer, the guy he'd been moving chairs with, said as they set out the last ones. 'Never expected a crowd this size. Anyone else who comes is going to have to stand at the back. Along with us.'

Families filled the grassy area in front of the stage. Older adults — and a couple of kids with broken legs — occupied the hundred or so chairs they'd set out already, and teenagers and young adults stood around the edges, joining in as cheerfully as if it was a rock concert.

The not-so-gentle scent of citronella wafted everywhere, with a sharp undertone of insect repellent spray. Owen squashed a mosquito on his wrist that apparently had no sense of smell. He didn't see many others about, fortunately. Not a mutation he wanted to see enter the gene pool.

The small band on the stage made it through the first verse and a chorus of Jingle Bells before the guitarist, a young Aboriginal guy, stopped playing and waved the others to stop. 'Whoa!' he said into the mike. 'What's all this about snow and sleighs? We got any of that about here, kids?'

'Adam's the local police constable, a good bloke,' Karl explained to Owen, as the audience laughed and roared a 'No!'

An Aboriginal police constable, and obviously well-liked. Owen noticed a number of Aboriginal family groups in the crowd, and although they seemed to stick together, there were white faces in among the dark, and vice-versa, and everyone seemed friendly and easy with each other. Not always the case in small communities, and it pleased him to see it.

'Yeah, I've never seen any snow here either,' the policeman guitarist said. 'So how about we have some Aussie carols, hey? If you don't know this one, it's on your song sheet. It's an old one but a good one.'

Owen recognized the tune from the introductory few bars, one of the Australian carols written in the 1950s that they'd still taught when he was at school. And as the band and the audience lifted up their voices to sing joyfully and vigorously about the north wind tossing the leaves, and the red dust over the town, it fitted this place, this community, with the bush around them on the other side of the curving creek, and the sun low in the rich blue sky.

'No north wind tonight,' Karl said quietly under the singing. 'But it's forecast for tomorrow. Straight down from outback Queensland. Fingers crossed there are no bushfires. Often bring trouble, those dry north winds.' But he joined in the singing on the chorus, gravelly and slightly off-key and oblivious to that in his enthusiasm.

Owen caught sight of Angie and her mother coming across from the hall, and he waved them over to one of the few empty chairs, holding it for Nancy Butler as she sat with a surprised thanks.

Angie sang in a light, clear voice, her eyes shining with pleasure and a challenge to him to sing, too. So he did, although it had been a long time since he'd sung anything and his voice probably sounded rustier than Karl's. But here it didn't matter and as he breathed properly and deeply through his diaphragm the increased oxygen flowed through his body, easing his jet lag and the underlying fatigue. And despite everything, despite injured children and empty shops and whatever else this community had been through, there was a kind of invigoration, of exhilaration in being part of a large group of people singing together in pure pleasure.

When the sun set a small choir sang a Christmas lullaby, and as their voices intertwined in a gentle harmony, everybody lit their candles, a sea of small flames lighting children's faces, wide-eyed in wonderment. Karl had matches, and Angie lit her candle from his, and passed on the wavering flame to her mother and Owen.

Owen wasn't religious and in his years of work overseas he'd seen no evidence of a benevolent deity, but after months of war and suffering, the ever-present tension – the wariness that life could be blown apart any moment – receded, and a something like a sense of relaxation settled in him.

After more rousing carols they finished with Silent Night, the candles shining like reflections of the stars in the vast clear sky. Angie, standing behind her mother, rested a hand on her shoulder, and Nancy clasped it, her small voice petering out into several sniffs. Angie softly sang on, her fingers closing more tightly around her mother's. Throughout the crowd, similar signs of affection, of tenderness, showed in children held gently; couples holding hands or leaning into one another; neighbours, families, lovers and friends sharing the quiet joy of being together and celebrating hope and love. It didn't matter whether it was Dungirri or Brisbane or Aleppo or Baghdad or wherever; that human capacity for hope and love was the same, and inspired courage and the will to overcome violence, fear and prejudice.

Angie's eyes shone in the candlelight and gratitude filled him. Whatever the next days and his grandfather's mystery brought, he was grateful for the experience of being here in Dungirri tonight.

In the stillness after the last notes of the carol sounded, the rumble of a truck approached. Flashing lights caught everyone's attention. For a fraction of a moment Owen tensed, until he recognised the excitement and expectation around him. Of course. A Rural Fire Service truck, with Santa in the front seat. When it pulled up and Santa descended, he was almost mobbed by children, but with a ringing bell in his hand he led them in to the hall like a Pied Piper, the adults trailing behind.

Owen didn't belong, he hardly knew anyone,

but he stayed for the supper in the hall, watching mostly from the side door open to the breeze while he enjoyed Nancy Butler's deliciously light lemon meringue pie. Although he searched the crowd for Philadelphia O'Connell, he didn't see her. But his gaze kept finding Angie, her bright print dress easy to spot in the crowd. She helped pass around supper plates and greeted people of all ages – people she'd probably known all her life – open and friendly, often with dry humour and good-natured teasing and being teased, but sometimes, too, with sympathy, and gentle hugs.

Despite everyone's efforts to be cheerful and the children's delight in Santa's gifts, evidence of the recent accident showed in a few kids still in plaster casts, one boy in a wheelchair, other kids sporting still-healing bruises and lacerations, and signs of strain in the faces of many parents.

The situation engaged his professional interest. What were the implications and issues for recovery from this scale of trauma in an isolated town? The nearest health services must be in Birraga, but it wasn't a large town either, and there wouldn't be much there, surely. Maybe a general practitioner or two. Maybe a physio or a counsellor if they were lucky. Not paediatric or orthopaedic specialists or trauma counsellors. They'd be hours away, in Tamworth or Dubbo. A long way to take a kid for check-ups, especially if juggling other siblings and work demands.

'We've met before, haven't we?'

He'd been watching Angie, and hadn't noticed

the woman's approach. Around his own age, with her hair drawn back in a ponytail from a serious, intelligent gaze. It only took him a moment to place her face. Jenn Barrett. Highly regarded journalist and foreign correspondent.

'We have. Last year in a refugee camp on the Syrian border with Lebanon. I'm Owen Caldwell.'

'Aha. Of course.' She shook hands firmly. 'Dungirri's a long way from Syria. What's brought you here?'

'I'm touring around with my grandfather,' he said simply. A tenacious, skilled journalist like her would be on to any hint of mystery in an instant. 'And you?'

'I grew up here. Seems as though Fate's given me some reasons to come back.' Her cheeks flushed lightly and her gaze darted from him to another man, deep in conversation nearby.

Another face he recognized, although he'd never met him. Mark Strelitz, recently resigned independent Federal politician. Interesting. Jenn Barrett and Mark Strelitz – two highly respected people with connections and influence, who probably knew how to get things done. Fortunate for Dungirri to have them.

'I heard about the bus accident,' Owen said. 'How is the town coping with the aftermath?'

'Hopefully funds raised tonight will help families with some of the immediate expenses.' She nodded towards the boy in the wheelchair. 'Cody's just come home from Tamworth hospital. Olly-' She indicated a kid standing rigid beside his mother, his face hidden in her dress, 'He hasn't slept the night through since the accident. The nearest child psychiatrist is in Dubbo. We're trying to get some longer-term support in place. But-' Her sharp eyes focused on him. 'The accident came on top of a heap of other issues. We sure could do with another GP in the district. There's only one in Birraga and she's already way overworked.' As if the hint wasn't unsubtle enough, she added, 'And at least half the guys here won't tell a woman doctor when they're struggling.'

Angie saved him from having to come up with an answer, bringing over a plate with three fruit mince tarts on it. 'I got the last of Jeanie's famous tarts,' she said. 'Lucky for us. Welcome home, Jenn. I see you've met Owen.'

'I have. A year or so back. In Syria.'

'Syria?' Angie shot the question to him but he'd taken a bite of the offered tart so he let Jenn answer.

'Yes. In a hell-hole of a refugee camp. I was just telling Owen that we could do with a doctor here.'

'You're a doctor.' Angie's mouth curved in approval. They'd exchanged no details about occupations, about anything much more than names. He'd found out little about her – other than her friendliness, the way people here liked her, the down-to-earth way she treated people, and the good-natured humour that said she didn't take herself too seriously. She tilted her head a little, curious. 'But what were you doing in Syria?'

He swallowed the delicious brandy-laced fruit and pastry. 'I've been working with Médecins Sans Frontières for a while. Doctors without Borders,' he added, because he usually mangled the French pronunciation, and some people didn't know the French name, anyway.

Distracted by someone, Jenn excused herself, taking one of the tarts with her.

'Good on you. I've always admired the work of MSF. Syria must have been a huge challenge. How long have you been back?'

He glanced at his watch and made a quick calculation. 'About sixteen hours.'

'Seriously? Wow. Your head must still be spinning with the contrasts. I sure hope Dungirri stays nice and quiet and boring for you.'

He didn't resist the smile. 'Oh, Dungirri's far from boring.'

Angie waited for a moment and glanced around before she asked in a low voice, 'Are you really interested in that guitar? Because if you are, Ryan and Beth could do with the money. Beth and the older girls were in the bus, and Beth's been off work since then because of her arm. She's run out of leave and Christmas is looking bleak. But don't you dare tell them I told you that.'

He didn't *need* a guitar, but yes, he wanted one again. The music from the band tonight still hummed along in his head. He 'd not bought anything for himself for ages, beyond the basics. And he could help out a family in need.

'I bought it years ago,' Ryan Wilson told him, when Angie took Owen over and introduced them. 'Didn't know the difference between classical and acoustic guitars.' He flushed a little. 'Thought I might teach myself but turns out I'm only good for songs with the kids. And this guitar's way too good for that. I picked up a cheap acoustic last year and it's fine for us.'

Owen's interest increased. 'I'm keen to take a look at it. When would suit you?'

'Come up now, if you like. We're heading home as soon as Beth rounds up the girls, and we're just a couple of blocks away.'

Ryan introduced him to his wife Beth, and their three daughters, the oldest nine or ten, the youngest about three. The girls were all shy, and tired, although they chatted quietly to each other while Owen strolled with the family up the road, the youngest crawling on to her father's lap in the wheelchair for the last part of the way.

They lived in an old house on the edge of town, opposite the bushland. Beth welcomed him inside and apologised for the mess but Owen saw nothing to apologise for – a warm, inviting home with books and pencils strewn on the coffee table and a Christmas tree in the corner, loaded with hand-made decorations.

When Beth brought the guitar case in and Owen opened it up, he knew he'd walk out with it. He wouldn't change his choices for a minute – studying medicine, working overseas – but music-making would always be an important part of him, a way to ground himself, and he'd neglected it for too long.

'Try it out,' Ryan said. 'I tuned it up as well as I could, but it's probably not perfect.'

Sitting on the couch, the guitar resting on his

thigh, Owen fingered the strings and tuned a couple more closely. He played a short study he'd learned in high school, an early nineteenth century piece he'd been fond of. His fingers found the notes easily, as though it hadn't been some years since he'd held a guitar, and the instrument had a beautiful tone, rich and resonant.

Absorbed in the piece, he didn't look up until the last notes faded, and found the Wilson family watching him in awe.

'It's yours,' Ryan said. 'I could never make it sound like that. You play brilliantly.'

'I studied classical guitar for a while,' he explained. 'This is a good instrument, a lovely tone.' He'd withdrawn a good amount of Australian currency at the airport this morning, uncertain where he'd next have access to his account, but the pub did have a cash machine so he paid Ryan for the guitar in cash, there and then, rather than a bank transfer. If he and Beth were short of funds for Christmas, the cash should help out tomorrow.

He strolled the couple of blocks back down to the pub with the guitar case slung on its strap over his shoulder, enjoying the warm night air and the quiet, rural streets.

In the courtyard, Angie, Karl, Adam and others had gathered around one of the large tables, Adam at the end with his guitar. Angie invited him to join them for a drink, and rolled off the names of the people he hadn't met yet. Lexi, Mel, Keisha, Eric, Luke . . . He repeated them in his head to help them stick.

Angie saw the guitar case on his shoulder and beamed. 'You bought it.'

'Yes.' At her insistence, and Adam's, he drew out the instrument.

'It's a good one,' Adam said. 'I had a look the other day. But I've got a couple already. What do you play?'

'Not much, lately. Mostly classical and jazz. But I was in a rock band for a mad few months in high school.'

Adam grinned. 'Jazz, hey? Pull up a chair, mate.'

Karl took orders for another round of drinks and Angie made room for him beside Adam. For half an hour or more conversation flowed around the table while he and Adam riffed off each other and improvised. Karl fetched a mouth organ from his car and proved to be a better musician than singer. When Adam grinned and morphed a riff into the opening bars of Macarena, Owen picked up the tune, Lexi and Angie dragged Keisha to her feet to dance, and everyone joined in and sang.

When the song finished, Owen regretfully returned his guitar to its case and said good night to everyone. Although not particularly late, he'd neglected his grandfather, and jet lag was dragging at him again.

Music still in his head, he whistled softly as he went up the stairs at the pub to check on his grandfather. An unexpectedly enjoyable evening. Despite being a stranger, he'd been made welcome, and he'd enjoyed the relaxing time with people who could become friends. And he loved the way Angie's eyes shone with pleasure, and the easy way she laughed. He hadn't laughed as much in . . . years.

But he found his grandfather sitting up in bed, propped up by pillows, his hand pressed to his chest, breathless and pale.

CHAPTER 3

Owen sat on the bed and took his grandfather's hand. 'Hey, what's up? I can see you're breathless. Are you fibrillating? Or is there pain?'

Bernard could diagnose himself as well as Owen could. 'Not painful. Some mild fibrillations. Couldn't get a good breath, lying down. So I sat up, ten minutes ago.'

Under Owen's fingers, the skin of his wrist was cold, the pulse weak and irregular. 'Is it easier to breathe, sitting up?'

'A little. I'll probably be fine in a few more minutes.'

No you won't. The hand he held in his was swollen. He'd bet Bernard's ankles were, too. Breathlessness, swelling, irregular heartbeat and fibrillations: all classic signs of congestive heart failure, which could easily, if they hadn't already, lead to pulmonary oedema. His grandfather's aortic heart valve, replaced twenty years ago, might be deteriorating further.

Owen hid his worry, aiming to remain calm and

objective. 'You saw your cardiologist recently, didn't you? Did she change any medications?'

'Two weeks ago. She was happy, didn't change anything.'

'I don't suppose you brought a stethoscope or blood pressure monitor with you?'

Bernard attempted a smile. 'No, lad. I don't carry them now.'

'I didn't bring mine, either.' He should have. Even though he'd gone straight from the airport to his grandfather's place, he should have gone via the storage shed and retrieved his kit, even if it would have meant delaying their flights to Dubbo. And he should have stayed with Bernard this evening, and kept a closer eye on him.

Should, should, should.

He found another pillow in the wardrobe and helped his grandfather sit up straighter. 'I'm going to go downstairs and ask if there's a good first aid kit in town. I won't be long at all.'

Bernard nodded, without wasting breath on words.

Owen descended the stairs so fast he didn't see Angie as she came out of the bar with another tray of drinks, and he almost bowled her over.

'How far away is the nearest ambulance?' he asked. 'And is there any oxygen in town?'

'Your grandfather?'

'Yes.'

'Liam,' she called back over her shoulder, 'Call an ambulance for Mr Chynoweth. Now.' She shoved the tray of drinks on to the hall table. 'The ambulance will come from Birraga Hospital. But Karl's still here and I'll call Beth. They're in the SES, and trained as community first responders. They've got some equipment in the truck. What's wrong with him? What do you need?'

Trained. Community first responder. Equipment. Owen's own pulse rate eased a fraction. 'Congestive heart failure. Maybe fluid on the lungs. I need stethoscope, oxygen, blood pressure monitor, pulse oximeter and ECG if there's one.' In his anxiety, he'd reeled off that list as if she medically trained. 'All the heart equipment,' he translated.

She laid her hand lightly on his arm. 'Oxygen, scope, blood pressure, pulse meter, ECG. Go back up to him. I know the SES kit includes oxygen. Karl and Beth won't be long.'

'Thanks.' He meant it, grateful for her calm focus and reassurance. They'd have oxygen soon. He'd be able to examine his grandfather properly, assess his condition more effectively. But Bernard would more than likely be spending the night in Birraga hospital. If he agreed to go. He *needed* to go to the hospital. For oxygen therapy, medications to reduce the fluid build-up and tests to determine his heart function.

Owen took the stairs back up, two at a time. His grandfather's Advanced Care Directive specified no resuscitation. They weren't at the stage yet – he *hoped* they weren't at that stage yet – but if they couldn't get him stabilized in the next twenty-four hours, if his heart couldn't function well enough to keep his lungs clear of fluid, they might get to that point sooner rather than later.

He paused for one moment with his hand on the door knob. It wouldn't happen. It couldn't happen. Not yet. He drew in a breath. He could deal with this, whatever happened. He had to.

~

The small crowd of friends around the table in the courtyard fell silent as Angie hurriedly explained the situation.

Karl grabbed his keys off the table. 'You'll phone Beth?' he checked as he headed for the gate. 'Tell her I'm getting the truck and will pick her up in less than five.'

Adam set aside his guitar. 'I'll get cars moved to make sure the ambulance can park up close. Let me know if you need anything else.'

Angie nodded, already dialling Beth Wilson's number. 'Beth, elderly gent with congestive heart failure here at the pub. It's Owen's grandfather. Owen's a doctor but he needs equipment and help. Karl will collect you in a couple of minutes.'

Despite her natural reserve, Beth had been doing first aid in the district since she was in high school. 'I'll be ready for him,' she said, matter of fact. 'Tell Owen we won't be long.'

Angie pocketed her phone. At the bottom of the stairway, she closed and locked the door into the front bar – there were plenty of other exits – to keep the area clear and to discourage curious eyes. She opened the door onto the street and propped it wide. One of the guys from the bar was already moving his ute out of the way.

Good. Access as clear as could be managed in a century-old, two-storey hotel. The ambulance officers were going to curse the absence of a lift, but at least the stairway was wide, the legacy of grander times. And there'd be people to help them carry Mr Chynoweth down.

Upstairs, the door of the room stood open. Owen spoke quietly, gently, as his grandfather coughed. Angie waited until the coughing eased. 'Karl and Beth are on their way – they'll be here in a few minutes. Is there anything I can get for you?'

Owen indicated the almost-empty glass on the table. 'Some water, please.'

Grateful to have something useful to do, Angie brought back a jug of water, then returned downstairs as the SES truck pulled in to help Karl and Beth carry equipment up.

Beth and Owen began talking medial terms straight away, while Karl unpacked a kit. Not needed, Angie left the room. At least another twenty minutes before the ambulance arrived. She left the pub at a quick pace, back to her mother's home. She had time to grab a change of clothes, and bring her car back. If Owen didn't go in the ambulance, she'd drive him in to Birraga. He might plan to drive himself, but stress on top of jetlag and night driving on roads he didn't know made a dangerous combination. She hoped he'd see that sense. And even if he did go in the ambulance, she'd drive in, stay in Birraga and drive him back, tonight, or in the morning, or whenever he was ready.

He was a mature adult and a doctor, he could manage alone, but from her glimpse of his grandfather, struggling to draw breath, she feared that Owen – that both of them – might need a friend tonight.

~

Birraga Hospital's emergency department was well-equipped for its size, except in the matter of staff. One doctor and two nurses struggled to deal with a labour in progress, a child with appendicitis, and an elderly woman who had fallen and hit her head.

The oxygen had eased Bernard's breathing a little, but Owen's main concern was the fluid build-up he could hear on his lungs, and the rising temperature. Bernard was conscious and responsive, but tired, and he mostly rested with his eyes closed, the oxygen mask obscuring half his face.

'We're both doctors,' Owen told the triage nurse when she came to do initial observations. Fiona, her name tag read.

Fiona wrapped the blood pressure cuff around Bernard's arm. 'Medical doctors?'

'General practitioners. Fellows of the college.' Owen took his MSF identify card with his qualifications listed from his pocket.

About to pump up the cuff, Fiona glanced at the ID. 'I wouldn't wave that around too much,' she said. 'Otherwise you might find yourself working all night. It's been flat out since my shift started, and

Morag's almost falling over with exhaustion.'

They both fell silent, watching the monitor. Fiona turned it so that Bernard could see it, too, a courtesy that Owen appreciated on his grandfather's behalf.

Both diastolic and systolic readings came out low. Lower than it had been in the ambulance.

Fiona reached into the trolley for a stethoscope and a hand-pump cuff. 'I'll do it again, Doctor Chynoweth, but manually this time,' she told his grandfather. 'I never entirely trust these machines.'

'Thank you,' Bernard whispered, and Owen echoed the thanks. The hands-on approach had distinct advantages over the electronic, particularly in being able to hear the pulse and its changes under pressure.

The readings still came out low.

'I'm going to do an ECG, Doctor Chynoweth,' Fiona said just as Owen was about to request it. 'I know the ambos did one, but that was an hour ago and we want a baseline of when you arrived here. Is that okay?'

Morag Cameron, the doctor, a petite, non-nonsense woman in her fifties, introduced herself and watched with Owen as the printed chart emerged from the ECG machine. She ordered blood tests and a chest X-Ray before excusing herself to return to the woman in labour.

Bernard dozed again after he returned from the small radiology department, so Morag invited Owen over to the nurses' station and shared her thoughts while she went over the X-ray and ECG results.

'The blood tests won't be back for a while – I've

had to call the path technician in to deal with all this lot-' she waved her hand at the row of full beds. 'But the ECG – see here – suggests that the aortic valve is weakening and the X-ray definitely shows some pulmonary oedema, and likely pneumonia. I'll contact his cardiologist in the morning, but for now I'm ordering an increase in his furosemide for the fluid, and antibiotics. You're happy with that?'

Grateful for her professional courtesy, he agreed. Exactly what he'd do. Not that they had many other options.

'Does your grandfather,' Morag asked gently, 'have an Advanced Care plan?'

'Yes. I don't have it in hard-copy but I can email it to you.' His breath caught slightly. What had been sensible and reasonable in the hypothetical took on new meaning now. 'He's specified no extreme measures, invasive procedures, or CPR. He told the paramedics this evening that those are his wishes.'

'Antibiotics?'

'We discussed that. He's okay with that if necessary. For now, anyway.' Because Bernard had unfinished business. He hadn't said as much, but he'd intimated it. Owen didn't want to think what his grandfather's decision would be after he'd said whatever he needed to say to Philadelphia O'Connell.

Morag added the medication order to his grandfather's notes. 'Good. I've got a bed free in the ward. I'm going to admit him. It will be quieter there than in here.'

'You've got your hands full here tonight.'

'Yes. But the boy will go in the rescue helicopter

when it arrives. It should be here soon. Nothing concerning in the CT scan for Mrs Bates, but we'll keep her in for observation.'

'And the obstetric case?'

'No time to get her anywhere. She's seven centimetres dilated already. Dubbo's almost two hours away and I'm not going to put her in the back of an ambulance for that long. But we've got no delivery suite or midwife, so the baby is going to be born here. Poor kid is alone, and terrified.'

A commotion broke out in the waiting room, shouts and bangs and the crash of a chair, and Morag pushed herself to her feet and rushed out. With a quick glance to check his grandfather still rested peacefully, Owen followed her.

A muscular young man, drug-affected or psychotic or both, struggled with two police officers, yelling obscenities about the ants crawling all over him.

Angie, returning with two cardboard coffee cups in her hands, slipped around the side of the room to keep out of the way, and Owen held the door into Emergency open for her. 'Can you sit with Granddad?' he asked, and she nodded.

Owen stood ready to assist if necessary, aware from experience how dangerous and aggressive some drugs made people. But the sergeant and her offsider managed to get their charge up against a wall.

'You're tripping, mate,' the female police sergeant said to him, in a calm, even tone to de-escalate the situation. 'The drugs are messing with your head. There aren't any ants, I promise you.'

'Jesus, Kris,' Morag murmured, 'This is the third one this week.'

'Yeah. This guy's not local but I want to find the bastard who's been pushing this crap in town. Okay, matey, just hold still and I won't cuff you. The doc's going to help you. I know your head's feeling weird, but you're safe. Just hold still.'

Morag approached the man slowly. 'My name is Morag. I'm a doctor. Will you tell me your name?'

'No. No. No name.' The man spoke rapidly. 'It's a fucking trick. No name. You can't get in my head. Not in my head. Get out of my head, fucking ant bitch.'

Owen moved around a little closer, keeping his distance so as not to interfere, assessing the man's condition from a distance. The guy's flushed face dripped with sweat, his pupils dilated. He rocked incessantly against the police officers' hold, his fingers constantly moving, scratching the air.

'We're not going to hurt you,' Morag said, speaking evenly over his continued muttering. 'Whatever you've taken has made you sick. We just want to help you, to make you feel better.'

Standard procedure for psychotic or aggressive patients: keep calm, aim to de-escalate the situation. But Owen's experiences were in a city hospital, with more staff and trained security officers and a room away from other people to take a high-risk patient to. Here they had only three staff and two cops, and a ward of vulnerable patients just beyond the door.

One of the nurses from the emergency room opened the connecting door, but at the same instant the woman in labour cried out in distress, loud in the momentary hush.

'No!' the man roared, abruptly pushing himself back off the wall with such force the police officers lost their grip. He spun around, elbowing the young policeman in the face. As the police sergeant reached for him he grabbed her by the arms and with tremendous drug-fuelled strength flung her hard into Morag, throwing both women into the rows of chairs in a screech of metal and plastic and gasps of shock and pain. Morag's head hit the edge of a chair with a sickening thump. The police sergeant swore, a gash on her arm already bleeding.

Two injuries shifted the priority from calming the patient to immobilising him so that he could harm no-one else. Alleviating the immediate danger had to come before seeing to the injured.

'Get five milligrams of midazolam,' Owen said to the nurse, as he circled around to keep the guy's attention on him. 'Keep the door closed and pass it through the reception window. And call a code black or whatever your protocol is here.'

The young nurse hesitated, her glance darting between him and Morag. 'But you're not-'

Struggling to rise over the upturned chairs, Morag lifted her head unsteadily. 'Five mills of midazolam, *now.*'

'*No!*' the guy shouted. He grabbed a chair, lifting it and swinging it around himself like a shield, and yelling at them to keep away. The police constable rushed in and tried to take the chair from him but was struck on the face by one of the metal legs and staggered backwards.

Owen risked a quick glance towards the two women. The police sergeant was on her knees, holding her arm awkwardly, clearly in pain, but she put herself between the guy and Morag, protecting her.

They both needed medical care urgently. Perhaps the young police constable, too, although he seemed okay, still standing, his hand reaching for some weapon on his equipment vest. Owen shook his head. No way did he want capsicum spray or taser used. Not if they could possibly avoid it. He signalled by tapping his finger on his shoulder, where the cop had his radio, for him to call for back-up, and pointing him to where he wanted the officer – between the man and the two women.

Keeping out of reach of the flailing legs of the chair, Owen edged step by slow, slow step to move the drugged man closer towards the reception window, talking gently all the time. 'My name is Owen. I'm just visiting here but I am a doctor. You don't want to hurt anyone, do you? If you put the chair down, I can help you.'

The man stood, breathing heavily, watching him, the chair raised to his shoulder. Owen took another slow step forward.

'Fucking bastard!' the man roared, and charged towards Owen, swinging the chair with force.

~

Birraga Hospital had few staff on night duty and

none of them hunky, muscular men. The registered nurse from the main ward barely reached Angie's chin. Fiona, the triage RN – Angie remembered her from high school – wasn't much taller and was caught up attending the woman in labour, who gave increasingly frequent and distressed cries.

The young, nervous nurse from Emergency finally had the injection of sedative ready, but as she approached the reception desk through the nurses' station, the psychotic guy outside shouted again, something crashed loudly and she retreated rapidly as the reception window shattered, sending shards of glass through into the nurses' station.

Angie, who had made herself useful reassuring the other patients, went to the trembling nurse's side. 'Did the glass hit you?'

'No. I don't think . . . ' She still held the syringe, shaking in her hand. 'He's mad. They don't feel pain. He'll get in and attack us all.'

'Not if we can get the sedative in to him,' Angie said. 'How long does this take to work?'

'It might not. It doesn't work for everyone. What if-'

Angie cut off the panicked question. 'Best case scenario? How long?'

'F-five to ten minutes.' Her eyes filled with tears and the panic of past trauma. 'I can't. I'm s-sorry. I can't go out there.'

The petite nurse from the main ward – her name-tag read Nina – took the syringe from her. 'It's okay, honey. You go down to aged care and send the staff there to help. And ask them to collect the spare bed from the ward. We'll handle this.'

Fiona left her patient and the two nurses and Angie hastily checked the situation through the shattered glass of the reception window. Owen and the policeman circled around the deranged man, ducking and weaving to dodge him and the chair he used as a weapon. In the corner, Kris Matthews the police sergeant huddled over the doctor, protecting her, both of them bloodied.

'Shit,' Fiona muttered. 'Nina, we're going to bring the doc and Kris inside. Angie, I need you to open and shut the door and help them inside. Nina, you'll have to triage. Angie, you go sit with Lissa, the maternity patient.'

'I can't deliver a baby,' Angie protested as they lined up by the door.

'You won't have to,' Fiona said, as airily as when she'd captained the school netball team and ordered some attacking strategy. 'She's at least half an hour away yet. Probably longer. Are we ready? Right, *now.*'

The guy shouted and changed direction when he saw the door open, but the moment of distraction gave Owen and the cop the chance to tackle him. They all crashed to the ground, and Fiona darted over and injected the sedative while they held him down. He swore and struggled but the three of them were able to pull his arms around to handcuff him. Owen straddled him, cradling his head to lessen the impact of the man's incessant pounding against the floor.

Nina and Kris helped Morag inside, on her feet but unsteady and leaning heavily on them both.

Blood oozed from Morag's head, and ran from a long gash in Kris's arm, her uniform shirt soaked.

With a last glance at Owen, Fiona and the still-struggling man, Angie closed the door and made sure the lock clicked into place. Fiona could open it with her passcode. Owen and the policeman could leave by the public exit if Fiona wasn't there.

If the sedative worked quickly, they'd be all right. But Angie still felt as though she'd abandoned them.

Another nurse had arrived with an empty bed, but both she and Nina set to work settling the doc onto the bed with a neck brace and assessing Kris. Angie hovered but Nina reinforced Fiona's directions. 'Can you keep the young woman company for a few minutes? Scrub your hands and arms well and put on a gown from that trolley.'

She passed by Doc Chynoweth's cubicle and paused to check on him. The heart monitor beeped rhythmically, the squiggles on the screen consistent. He must have heard her because he opened his eyes.

'Are you doing okay?' she asked him.

He nodded. 'Yes. Where is Owen?'

'He's helping the staff. An incident with an aggressive patient. But everything's fine now. I'm sure he'll be back soon.'

He nodded again, his eyes drifting closed.

The elderly lady who'd had a fall appeared to have slept through the ruckus. The boy with the troublesome appendix lay awake, but whatever they'd given him for pain appeared to be working. 'Can you hear it?' he asked. 'I think the chopper is coming.'

Angie listened for a moment but heard nothing beyond the machines and the man struggling in the waiting room. 'If it is, we'll know for sure in a minute. Are your Mum or Dad around?'

'Mum went home to get some clothes. She'll be back soon.'

'Good-o.' He seemed content enough so she left him with a wave. 'Enjoy your chopper ride.'

Angie scrubbed diligently and pulled the blue gown over her clothes, but she stopped outside the curtains surrounding the young woman. What the hell did she know about childbirth? Nothing. Nothing beyond the most basic theory. And maybe one or two scenes on TV, which probably bore absolutely no relationship to reality. And she'd never met this young woman.

She should tell Nina that someone else would have to do it . . .

A sob came from behind the curtain, and another. Nina and the other nurse were flat out. Morag could be critically injured and Kris's arm dripped blood on to the floor. The drugged guy still yelled and thrashed outside, but not as loudly. The baby wasn't going to come yet.

Angie sucked in a deep breath and slipped through the curtain into the cubicle.

The young woman – Lissa, Fiona had called her – couldn't have been more than twenty years old, probably several years younger. Her face strained and damp from sweat and tears, she twisted the sheet in tight fists as a contraction gripped her.

Angie put a hand over Lissa's, and hoped her smile

looked more encouraging than panic-stricken. What was she supposed to do? Wipe sweat off her face? Or was that only in movies? Tell her to breathe? To puff hard? To push? Not to push?

'You're doing great,' she said, as useful as a waterproof teabag.

Half an hour yet. No need to panic. Just keep her company. For a few minutes.

She introduced herself as soon as Lissa's contraction eased. 'My name's Angie. The nurses have to deal with a couple of urgent patients, but they'll be back soon. Would you like me to sit with you?'

The girl – she was a girl, just a teenager – gripped her hand, searched her face and must have trusted what she saw. 'I'm scared. So scared.'

Without letting go of that desperate hand, Angie hooked a chair with her foot to bring it closer so that she could sit beside the bed. 'It's natural to be a bit scared of the unknown. But it's okay – Fiona will be back. She wouldn't have left you if she was at all worried.'

'All the noise out there – what's happening? Is the doctor hurt?'

'A guy took the wrong drugs and became a bit aggressive. The doc had a fall and hit her head but she'll be okay.' A hope more than a certainty, but she spared Lissa that worry. 'There's another doctor here and he'll come and see you soon, I'm sure.' And that was a presumption, but Owen had worked for MSF for years, and he didn't strike her as the kind of man who'd ignore a patient in need, even if he wasn't on the staff of the hospital.

She could definitely hear the helicopter now. Within minutes there'd be at least one more paramedic, and maybe extra police as well to guard the drugged guy.

The pain of another contraction contorted Lissa's face. It couldn't have been more than two minutes since the last one. She cried out, her breath coming in rapid huffs. 'Have . . . to . . . *push!*'

Angie's own heart pounded and with her free hand she pressed the call button before she perched on the bed, rubbing Lissa's back as the contraction took over her body. Angie tuned out the voices in the background and the one in her head muttering about her own lack of experience. Nothing mattered more than reassuring this girl that she wasn't alone. 'That's it. You're doing great. You can do this. You're brave and strong.'

She kept murmuring encouragement and holding her and massaging her through the pain. As it seemed to ease a little, the curtains parted slightly and Fiona slipped in, her hair dishevelled and a reddening mark on her cheek, but briskly tying on a clean gown over her scrubs. 'How are you going, love? Those contractions are getting close together, aren't they? Is it okay if I take a look to see how your baby's doing?'

As Fiona pulled on gloves for the very personal examination, Angie asked Lissa, 'Would you like me to go?'

Lissa's fingers tightened around hers. 'No. Please . . . please stay. If you can.'

That she could be so desperate for a stranger's presence at such a time raised a hundred questions that would have to wait. Whatever Lissa's story, Angie couldn't desert a frightened, vulnerable young woman.

'I can stay.' Angie checked with Fiona, 'As long as Mr Chynoweth doesn't need me?'

'He's been resting. Owen's just checked on him. He's doing okay.'

'Good.' While Fiona conducted her examination, Angie offered Lissa some chips of ice in a plastic cup. 'I'll stay with you, honey, as long as you want me to. But I've not had a baby, so you tell me what you want me to do, okay? Imagine I'm your sister and boss me around.'

Tears welled in Lissa's eyes. 'My sister wouldn't help me,' she whispered.

Damn, damn, damn. Wrong thing to say. 'Well, I'm here, Lissa, and I will.'

No woman could look herself, let alone poised and mature, in a hospital gown with damp hair plastered about her face, breathing heavily from pain. As Angie helped her into a more comfortable position, it struck her how young Lissa was. Young, and skinny under the folds of cotton fabric. Maybe not so much skinny as wiry, but not a gram of fat on her, the bulge of the baby huge on her slim frame. How could a sister not help her?

'You're in transition, Lissa,' Fiona said. 'The baby's moving from your womb into the birth canal. That's why your contractions are coming so quickly. This is the hardest phase, but it won't last long. You move around however you need to. Try to relax between contractions.'

Angie wasn't sure if the explanation of the process was for her benefit or not, but Lissa had only one question. 'Is the baby all right?'

'Yes. The baby's heart beat is nice and strong, and your labour is going normally. Everything's good. I just have to see to another patient but I'll be back in a few minutes, okay?'

In the background, Angie caught snippets of a quiet discussion between Morag and Owen, Morag's Scottish accent carrying a little further than his low voice. '. . .*homeless* . . .' '*Limited ante-natal care*'. '*Brave kid . . . did her best to look after her health . . .*'

Homeless. The dusty backpack and the small red and white checked bag on the floor at the foot of the bed took on more significance, but Angie had no time to ponder more as Lissa gasped in pain and the next contraction began.

When that one passed and Lissa sat panting on the edge of the bed, Owen came into the curtained-off cubicle. He wore a hospital gown over his jeans and t-shirt, the blue of the fabric making his eyes seem more blue than grey. Angie saw no sign of injury, and she breathed a little easier.

He greeted Lissa and introduced himself. 'I'm not on the staff here, but Doctor Cameron has had a bang on the head and it's important that she lies down and rests for a while, as a precaution. She's asked me to help out, because there aren't any other doctors in town. I'm a general practitioner, not a specialist, but I've had a good deal of obstetric experience. Are you happy if I help to deliver your baby?'

Angie liked the quiet, respectful way he spoke to Lissa, giving her the agency to decide. When Lissa nodded her agreement, Owen laid a gentle hand on her wrist. 'That's good. Doctor Cameron told me that you've asked for a natural birth, without pain assistance. The contractions in this stage of labour can be very intense and long, so if you change your mind, you just ask, okay?'

'No drugs,' Lissa insisted. 'Unless . . . unless the baby needs them. I don't want to hurt it. You'll tell me if the baby needs it, won't you?'

'I promise I will.' He might have said more but her eyes widened with the beginning of another wave of pain, and he encouraged her to push while Angie held her tight and wished she could absorb some of the discomfort to spare her. Lissa's courage and her determination to do the best for her baby impressed her.

Although Fiona came and went several times, Owen stayed, his presence calm, focused and always respectful of Lissa, explaining in clear non-medical terms what was happening, asking permission before examining her.

In one short lull, while Lissa lay back against her shoulder and Angie tried to breathe evenly with her, she caught Owen's eye. He smiled at her, weary but with the warmth of shared experience, of friendship and liking.

Funny that this afternoon she'd stopped to say hello in passing to a stranger in town, and now they worked together to help another stranger bring a tiny human into the world.

Everything she'd seen of him she liked and respected. In these past few hours, packed with intensity, he'd demonstrated professionalism, courage, and kindness. Not to mention a reassuring lack of ego. If it hadn't been for his acquaintance with Jenn Barrett, she'd have known nothing about his work for MSF. No casual mentions of 'When I was in Syria . . .' or other bragging. Unlike some of her male colleagues, who peppered their conversations with 'When I did that survey for Santos . . .' or Rio Tinto, or Hancock Prospecting or some other big-name company or project. The old *my project is bigger than yours* game.

The minutes ticked by, and an hour, and as each contraction gripped Lissa and she strained with every muscle in her body, Angie reminded herself that thousands of women did this every day, and that Owen's reassurances to Lissa revealed no worry or anxiety. Trusting in Owen's experience, she concentrated on the girl, on being there for her, giving her support and strength and encouragement.

When the baby crowned Angie's own breath caught in her throat. 'Almost there, Lissa,' she murmured.

'Now, some little pushes for the baby's head,' Owen instructed. 'Nice and easy. That's good. That's right. Now stop pushing for a moment while I check the position of the cord.'

Angie could only see the back of the baby's head. 'Your baby has a lot of dark hair,' she told Lissa. 'Not long to go.'

'Everything's fine,' Owen said, with a genuine smile at Lissa. 'Now a few more strong pushes . . .'

The baby arrived with a small wail of protest into Owen's gentle hands, and after he quickly cleared some mucus from the little open mouth, he placed her on Lissa's chest. 'Meet your daughter, Lissa.'

Although Fiona stepped forward to put a towel around the baby and run through the checklist of observations, and Owen attended to the umbilical cord, neither of them interfered with Lissa's first embrace of her daughter.

Tears ran down Lissa's face as she held the child against her skin, touching the small screwed-up face and the soft dark hair with wonder.

'She's so beautiful,' she whispered. 'So tiny. Hello, my little girl.'

Her own happy tears blurring her vision, Angie tucked another pillow behind Lissa's back to support her more comfortably as Fiona gently rubbed the baby and cleared a little more mucous from her nose, resulting in another plaintive wail and wriggling limbs.

'Ssh, ssh, baby,' Lissa soothed. 'It's all right.' She cast a worried glance to Fiona. 'It is, isn't it?'

'Yes. Crying helps her to clear her lungs. Her responses are very good. Keep talking and holding her. She knows your voice.'

Angie stepped back, out of the way, her job done. The baby's hand curled around her mother's finger as Lissa murmured her love and assurances, her words punctuated by small sobs.

Lissa raised her teary face to the three of them

watching. 'I can't give her up,' she said. 'Please don't take her from me. Please don't let them take her from me.'

CHAPTER 4

Lissa didn't entirely believe either him or Fiona that they had no intentions of taking her baby. Owen's assurances that the social worker would connect her with support services to help her met with a doubtful nod and a bleakness that shouldn't be in the eyes of a teenager. But she was homeless, which meant the system had already failed her.

After the placenta was delivered and the post-birth checks completed, Angie promised to stay with Lissa, so he left his patient in that capable company for now. As he studied Morag's CT scans, he could hear the quiet murmur of Angie's voice, drawing Lissa's story from her with compassion and understanding.

The radiologist was located in Dubbo and his report wouldn't be available until at least eight in the morning, after he'd viewed the scans online. In a larger hospital, in a city, it wouldn't take that long. Owen looked closely at the images, both on the digital files and on the film, searching for any sign that Morag had suffered a skull or brain injury that needed more urgent action. He didn't find anything, but he took the films to her so that she could examine them herself if she wished.

She spent a few moments squinting at them against the light in a cursory examination before she handed them back. 'I can't see anything of concern.' She lay back against the pillows and shaded her eyes. 'I'm sure I will be perfectly fine. I've had the migraine for two days now. It's not new. I should get up and get back to work.'

The dark circles under her eyes and the sensitivity to light argued against that idea, despite the reduced likelihood of significant injury. Owen suspected over work and exhaustion contributed to the migraine.

'You should stay where you are and have hourly obs, until we have the radiologist's report.' He cut off her protest. 'There's no-one who needs anything now other than monitoring. The nurses will do that. If anything urgent comes up, I'll be here with my grandfather. So close your eyes and get some well-deserved rest.'

Her wan smile signalled capitulation to good sense – or to the pain of the migraine. 'Are you registered with a locum agency?' she asked.

'Yes.' He told her which one. 'But my status is listed as unavailable just now.'

'Change it. I'll see what I can work out about getting you paid for tonight.'

'I'm not doing it for the money.'

'I know. But it's better if we make can make it official. I'll ensure it's documented that you acted on my instructions.'

In case any issues arose. 'Thanks, Morag. But I'm happy to stand by my own decisions.'

'Of course.' She watched him write a note on her chart and initial it. 'If you're looking for a job, let me know. We're pretty desperate out here.'

He could see that. One GP, for clinic practice and emergency on-call. No-one else for over a hundred kilometres. The work would certainly be varied . . . 'Granddad lives in Brisbane,' he said, before any tendrils of temptation could take root in his thoughts. 'I'll have to stay close to him.'

But the idea stayed with him, floating on the edge of his thoughts as he checked on Mrs Bates – sleeping peacefully – and the drug-affected man, not exactly sleeping or peaceful but quiet enough, and under the guard of a burly police officer. Out in the waiting room, the police sergeant spoke on the phone, giving instructions to her colleagues, the arm he'd sutured for her in a sling. But she finished her call as a man arrived – the man Owen had seen at the pub the previous afternoon – and as he came through the door she walked in to his embrace. Owen turned away from the private moment.

Almost three o'clock in the morning. Nothing more for him to do. Angie still talked quietly with Lissa. Fiona had not long finished a round of observations and emerged from the curtain around his grandfather's bed. Owen quietly pulled aside the curtain again and found Bernard still awake, half-sitting supported by pillows and the angled bed. A glance at the monitors showed that heart-rate, oxygen saturation and blood-pressure had improved a little further in the last hour or so.

As Owen pulled a chair closer, Bernard slipped the oxygen mask down and asked, 'The mother and baby – everything is all right?'

'Yes. No complications, and they're both doing well.' No complications other than a young mother, alone in the world and traumatised, apparently, by her experiences of social welfare. Owen's elation at witnessing a healthy birth hadn't lasted long in the face of her fear.

'I'm glad,' Bernard murmured.

Owen nodded. They'd discussed childbirth once, not long after he'd graduated. *It is the best thing imaginable,* his grandfather had told him, *to see a healthy child born. But it is the worst thing imaginable to lose a child at birth.*

The best and worst . . . Owen now had years of experience of both to agree. Except he'd add a rider – even worse for a baby to die through the violence of bombs or starvation or lack of basic medical facilities.

His muscles began to relax into the relative comfort of the chair but he kept his eyes resolutely open. He wanted to see Angie, as soon as she left Lissa. If she didn't emerge from the cubicle soon, he'd go and check that they both had everything they needed.

'Owen . . .' His grandfather reached out a hand to him and Owen leaned forward to take it. 'I must ask you . . . to do something for me.' The oxygen mask still hung around his neck, not helping his breathing.

'The briefcase… Please take that to Miss O'Connell. In the morning. Tell her it is all explained . . . in the letter. Tell her that I do not expect her forgiveness . . . But I am deeply sorry for the wrong I did her.'

'You'll be on your feet again in a day or so, Granddad. You can tell her yourself.'

'No. Please lad, please see her. In the morning. It's important.'

'Can you tell me what this is about? Before I see her?'

'I can't, lad. It is for her to tell . . . if she chooses to do so.'

Mystery on mystery, but Bernard, usually so calm, gripped his hand tightly, begging him with his eyes.

'Okay,' Owen assured him. 'I promise I'll go and take the briefcase to her. Now let me fix that mask for you.'

His grandfather settled back with the mask in place. His oxygen saturation began to improve again and after a few minutes he dozed off.

Owen rose quietly and went in search of a glass of water. In a few hours – later this morning – he'd fulfil his promise to his grandfather and visit Philadelphia O'Connell. He hoped that whatever Bernard had on his conscience would turn out to be some small matter, easily resolved and of no consequence. He couldn't imagine his grandfather ever doing a significant wrong to anyone.

~

Lissa lay on her side on the bed, watching her tiny daughter sleeping. Angie left her to get some rest, hopeful that their long discussion had alleviated at least some of the girl's immediate worries.

Owen, leaving his grandfather's cubicle, signalled for her to join him and she followed him in to the small staff kitchen.

Closing the door, he asked, 'How is Lissa?'

Tiredness dragged at her and she stifled a yawn. 'She's calmer,' she said, when she had air in her lungs again. 'She's had a shower and I persuaded her to have a sandwich. I think she'll sleep for a while now.'

'Good. I'm glad you were there.' He found two glasses in a cupboard and filled them from the water cooler. 'Did she tell you much?'

Angie accepted the offered glass and pulled out a chair at the small table. 'She's just turned seventeen years old. She's been a ward of the state since she was five. She ran away from her seventh foster home two years ago, when her foster-father began abusing her. She's lived in refuges and on the streets since then.'

Owen grimaced. 'The system fails too many kids, sadly. The father of the baby?'

'A guy she loved, another homeless kid, same age as her. He battled with depression and stepped out in front of a train before she knew she was pregnant.'

He closed his eyes for a moment. 'She's had a rough time.'

'Yes.' Angie took another sip of the cooling water to wet her dry throat. 'She had a job for a few months, cleaning in a caravan park on the north coast, but the owner sacked her when she started getting big. And didn't pay all her wages. She went looking for her older sister in south-east Queensland – they were separated years ago – but the sister is married to an alcoholic no-hoper who wouldn't let Lissa stay.'

'Does she have anyone else she can go to? Family? Friends?'

'No family, other than the sister. Mum dead from overdose, father unknown. But the reason she came here, to Birraga – she hitched from Queensland – was because there's a girl she met on the streets in Sydney who lives in Dungirri now.'

'Do you know her?'

'Did you meet Gil Gillespie at the pub?'

He obviously didn't see the connection, but answered the question. 'Tall dark guy in the courtyard this afternoon? He came in to pick up the police sergeant not long ago.'

She couldn't help but smile at that news. Kris and Gil. Kris wouldn't have asked him to drive sixty kilometres and back in the small hours of the morning unless the rumours of a relationship were true. 'That will be him. It's a long story, but he has a daughter, Megan. She was working at the pub tonight, too.'

'The teenager in the kitchen uniform? I only saw her briefly.'

'Yes. Megan's mother gave her up for adoption at birth, but her adoptive parents were killed in an accident a couple of years back. Things didn't work out after that and she spent some time homeless on the streets of Sydney before Community Services located her natural grandparents, and she came to Dungirri to live with them.'

And with fatigue fogging her brain that was probably a rambled explanation but Owen seemed to get the general gist. 'And Gillespie?'

'Didn't know she existed until he came back to town a couple of months ago.'

'Must have been some shock. How did he respond to that?'

'He's a decent man under that gruff exterior. Kris wouldn't give him the time of day if he wasn't. And Megan's a good kid. She and Lissa stuck together in Sydney because they both wanted to steer clear of drugs and prostitution. Which is why Lissa came down this way looking for her. Megan's her only friend. But her labour started before she could get to Dungirri.'

'But if Megan's only a teenager herself,' he asked, 'what can she do to help?'

'Be a friend. Lissa doesn't have anyone else who knows her. Poor kid is aching with loneliness. I'll call Megan in a few hours. I'm sure someone can bring her in.'

'The nursing staff will contact the social worker tomorrow, but I guess services probably can't move fast at this time of year.'

Angie agreed. Christmas Eve, when many services were shut by lunchtime for several days, if not until after the New Year. 'When do you think she'll be discharged?'

'I won't be the one making the decision. But

she and the baby are both doing well. So perhaps tomorrow or the next day. Although if she has nowhere to go, they might be able to keep her in a little longer.'

A newborn baby with a homeless, inexperienced young mother . . . despite Lissa's determination to do her best for her baby, she had a tough road ahead. Social services might be able to find her emergency housing and some cash, but she'd need so much more than that.

'It's Christmas time,' Angie said, choosing optimism over worry. 'What better time to help a homeless baby and her mother? We'll find a way to look after them until community services can help her.'

'We?'

'Dungirri has been through a lot but the people – they're good people. As soon as it's a decent hour I'll make some phone calls. I know some women who make things happen. We'll find somewhere for her to stay. If nothing else comes up, she can stay at the pub. And I'm sure Beth will be happy to advise her on baby matters.'

She thought of the women in Dungirri. Her mother. Jeanie Menotti. And the other women who'd arranged the supper and the Christmas tree. Beth, using her first aid skills for years. The women who always stepped up to help were often the backbone of their communities. Even reclusive Delphi O'Connell could be relied on to lend a hand wherever it was needed.

Another yawn caught her and she screwed up her

face as she tried and failed to suppress it. She caught the amusement in his eyes and her answering grin battled with her yawn for control of her features. She must look ridiculous. Especially under this harsh fluorescent light at three in the morning. She didn't care.

'You should go home, and get some sleep,' he said, when her yawn died away.

'Not much point driving so far when I'd just have to come back again. I'll snooze in an armchair. That way I can be there for Lissa when she wakes up. I assume you're staying, too?'

'Yes. Just in case anyone throws complications. Morag needs rest and observation. I told her I'll stay until morning, so that she doesn't have to do anything.'

'Will you sleep?' Angie asked him.

'Yes.' He made an effort to be light-hearted. 'First thing you learn at med school: how to sleep almost anywhere.' He pushed himself to his feet, collecting both their empty glasses to refill them at the cooler.

Her back stiff from sitting awkwardly in a chair beside Lissa for so long, she rose too, and propped herself against the counter near him. 'Will your grandfather be okay?'

No. He didn't say the word aloud, but she read it in his face, and in his pause before he answered.

'His heart is failing,' he said. 'He should pick up with the antibiotics and diuretics, for now. But . . . he's ninety in a few days. And I think he's almost ready to let go.'

She touched her hand to his arm. 'I'm sorry,

Owen. You're very close to him, aren't you?'

'Yes.' Just that one word, before he swallowed heavily.

She filled the silence so he didn't have to. 'It's good that you're able to spend this time with him.'

He gave a half shake of his head. 'I should have spent more time with him. I've been overseas so much. We've all been away. He has no-one but my siblings and me and we've left him alone too long.'

Regrets. She carried a truckload of her own. Going hiking in New Zealand last Easter instead of coming back to see her folks. The next time she'd seen her Dad, he'd been hooked up to life support, his brain dead from a massive stroke, his ever-cheerful spirit already gone. Only the shell of him, unable to hear that she loved him, unable to hear her goodbye.

'You're here with him now. That matters.' *And I'm home with my Mum for Christmas.* Her shy, hard-working, under-confident, devoted, neglected mother. She had to ensure she made this time with her mother matter, too.

Owen leaned a hip against the counter. Despite the early hour – maybe because of it – there was an easiness between them. 'He's been there for me for most of my life. My dad died when I was eleven. Granddad moved in with us to help Mum. When Mum died, I was eighteen and just starting uni. Between us, Granddad and I looked after my brother and sister. I couldn't have done that, and studied, without him.'

So much more to this man than simply an attractive face. 'Losing both your parents so young must have been hard,' she said. 'Your siblings are lucky to have you.'

'It wasn't easy, but we were fortunate. My parents had professional careers. We had a home, we had few financial concerns, and we had my grandfather. Those are privileges that too many people don't have. Like Lissa.'

Like Lissa, with a long road ahead of her and no resources and no family to fall back on. 'She has a strong sense of herself and a great deal of courage,' Angie said. 'That's a good start, as long as it can be nurtured.'

'Yes. And she has kept herself healthy, which helps her and her baby.'

Avoiding drugs and alcohol, and trying to eat good food. Angie had a great deal of respect for her.

'I've never been at a birth before. It was . . .' she couldn't find a suitable word. Amazing? Awesome? 'Incredible,' she settled on, although that was inadequate for the way the experience had moved her. Before she choked up again, she added, 'Particularly since I didn't have to do the pushing. But I guess you've seen heaps.'

His smile softened his face. 'It doesn't matter how many. A healthy birth is always wonderful. And the biology of it is mind-blowing.'

'Sperm meets ovum, and nine months later – wow.' Damn, not the most intelligent response. And thinking about how sperm meet ova, when she was standing at three-ish in the morning within touching distance of a decidedly gorgeous man, brought a wave of heat to her face. So much for being a confident, almost thirty-year-old professional woman. Blushing like a thirteen-year-old at the mere thought of sex.

'Yes. Wow.' His eyes sparkled, as if he knew exactly where her thoughts had gone. Of course he did.

She drained her glass of water. It didn't help. So she busied herself washing it at the sink and not looking at him. 'Thanks for everything you did tonight. It would have been chaos here, without you. Birraga's desperate for another doctor. The last guy only stayed a couple of months.' And there she went, prattling again.

She felt his hand, warm on her shoulder. 'Thank *you*, for all your help. For driving me here. For staying with Lissa. You were brilliant with her. Calm and supportive and caring. Just what she needed.'

'I just wanted to help.' *I just want that hand on my shoulder to draw me into a close hold and to put my arms around you* . . . Three in the morning. Not a good time to make decisions about intimacy with a man you'd only recently met. Even if it was only a hug. Even if the man was Owen Caldwell, a sane, caring, compassionate man who'd worked half the night on top of jet lag and might appreciate a hug himself.

She touched her hand to his and stepped away. 'We should both go and get what sleep we can,' she said.

Yet as she curled up in an armchair near Lissa's bed and pulled a cotton blanket over her shoulders she almost wished she'd given in to temptation. Being close on thirty and all responsible and sensible was no fun. But her mother would be proud of her.

~

Owen splashed his face with cold water in the old-fashioned bathroom at the pub. Eight-thirty in the morning, and showered, dressed, shaved. And mostly awake. The couple of hours of broken sleep he'd managed at the hospital – and the half hour in the car while Angie drove him back to Dungirri – would have to do for now.

Back in his room, his grandfather's briefcase sat on the floor beside the table. Heavy, he discovered, when he lifted it to the table. He flicked the catches open. An envelope addressed to Miss P. O'Connell sat on the top of a number of hardcover journals and albums. In spite of his curiosity, Owen didn't move anything. He closed the briefcase up and left it there while he went downstairs in search of some breakfast. It would be best to have something to eat before he went out. Dungirri had few options for food outside the pub's limited meal times.

Breakfast was laid out in the bistro, a basic self-serve array of cereals, fruit, yoghurt, and options for toast and spreads. And coffee. Plunger coffee with a choice of grounds. He made his strong.

He saw no-one while he ate his hurried breakfast, although as he finished an older woman in an apron came out from the kitchen. The woman he'd seen yesterday with Philadelphia O'Connell. She'd also been at the hall last night, organising the food and the Christmas tree.

She came across to clear his table and enquired if

he wanted anything else. Polite and friendly, although her direct gaze studied him more closely than casual acquaintance.

'It's Owen, isn't it?' she asked. 'My name is Jeanie Menotti. I heard about your grandfather. I hope he's okay?'

Dungirri, like most small towns, clearly had an efficient social news network. 'Yes. He's doing much better.'

'Let us know if there's anything you need. Anything we can do to help.'

Because of the way gossip could travel, he debated with himself before asking, 'I think you know Philadelphia O'Connell?' A fairly safe question, given she was out there yesterday.

Her eyes narrowed, not exactly suspicious, but definitely cautious. 'Delphi? I'm staying with her at present. Why?'

Staying with her. Obviously friends. 'Is it too early to call on her now?'

'Delphi is up with the birds. She might be out in the paddocks by now. What's your business with her?'

'My grandfather has asked me to take some-' Documents? Journals? How should he describe the contents of the case? 'Some information to her. He knew her a long time ago. But he will be in hospital for a couple of days, most likely.'

Jeanie considered him for a long moment. Perhaps she thought him dangerous, or was simply rightly cautious of a man going out to see an elderly woman on an isolated farm. 'What is your grandfather's name?'

Now he watched her closely. 'Chynoweth. Doctor Bernard Chynoweth.' An unusual name, but if she'd ever heard her friend mention it, she gave no sign of recognition at all.

'I'll call and tell her you're coming.'

'Thank you. I'd appreciate that.'

She paused, his used dishes still in her hands. 'Delphi is a good, hard-working woman, highly respected in this district. I trust you do not intend her any harm.'

'My grandfather is a good man, too. I don't know what this is about, but I know he would never wish to hurt anyone. Nor do I.'

On his way back to his room, he met Gillespie on the stairs. The man gave him a brief nod but passed without conversation. A decent man under the gruff exterior, according to Angie. Owen didn't mind. He wasn't feeling much like idle conversation himself.

Within a few minutes he was on the road to the O'Connell place, the case on the passenger seat beside him. He found the farm again without difficulty, remembering the machinery shed a short distance before the entrance to the farmhouse. This time, he turned across the cattle grid into the driveway, and parked behind the old utility she'd driven to town yesterday.

She waited for him on the veranda, standing there watching him as he walked towards her, saying nothing. She was dressed in work clothes; faded jeans, an equally faded denim shirt over a t-shirt, and dusty leather boots. A mottled grey and tan cattle dog stood at her feet, alert and focused on him.

'Miss O'Connell, my name is Owen Caldwell.' He held out his hand but she didn't move to shake it. Fair enough. He forged on with his explanation. 'My grandfather has asked me to bring you this briefcase. He would have come himself but he was taken ill last night, and is in the hospital.'

Her grey eyes studied him, wary, assessing. He couldn't read what she thought. The disconcerting sense of familiarity flickered through his mind again, but he couldn't pin it down. He'd have remembered this woman, her strong face lined with character and a lifetime of hard work.

'Jeanie said you were coming. She said you're Doctor Chynoweth's grandson?'

'Yes.'

Her eyes closed briefly, just once, and she made a small sound in her throat. But then those grey eyes opened and stared in to his again. 'Do you know why he came here?'

'No. He hasn't told me. He just asked me to bring you this briefcase. There's a letter inside. He said to tell you that he's deeply sorry, but he does not expect your forgiveness.'

He held out the case. Her hands tightened into fists at her sides as though she fought against the desire to take it. He set it down on the veranda between them. And waited.

'Where is your mother?' she asked abruptly.

The question took him by surprise. 'My mother? I'm afraid she died some years ago.'

She moved quickly, lifting the case and turning

away, reaching for the door handle. 'I have to fix some fencing,' she said in a rush. 'Come back after lunch.' But just as suddenly she stopped, the screen door held open, and although a fly buzzed around it she made no move to wave it off. She simply stood, her back to him, and her voice cracked when she asked, 'Your mother – was she happy?'

'Yes. She loved her work. She loved my father. We were – are still – a close family. My brother and sister and I still miss her.'

He thought he saw her shoulders shake, but she took rapid steps inside, the screen door whacked against the door frame, and the main door thumped closed.

He hesitated on the veranda, uncertain what to do. Knock and make sure she was okay? No. She'd said to call back later. And she had a friend in Jeanie at the pub, if she needed someone to talk to.

The dog still stared at him, a guardian at the door.

He returned to his car. He'd promised to see his grandfather this afternoon. He could come back and see Delphi first.

But Delphi's reference to his mother gnawed at him. She'd not asked after his grandfather, only his mother. He'd assumed, from the little Bernard had said, that there was some long-ago relationship – romantic or otherwise – between him and Delphi.

Instead of turning east to Dungirri at the end of the driveway, he turned west back to Birraga.

He'd go back to the hospital, tell his grandfather that he'd seen her, and ask what this was all about.

~

Nancy eyed Angie over the rim of her teacup. 'You've only just met him. But you stayed out all night with him.'

Her brain foggy from being awake much of the night, Angie rested her elbows on the kitchen table and took a sip of strong sweet tea to fortify herself for the discussion. 'At the hospital, Mum. With a whole lot of other people around. It was so crazy busy we both had to help out.'

'He's a doctor, you say?'

'Yes. And a good one.' She summarised the events of the night, although she skimmed over being present at the birth of the baby. That might distract her mother into contemplating Angie's impending thirtieth birthday and lack of babies. Far better to give her something practical to focus on, with a request for her help. She explained about Lissa's homelessness. She'd already planned who she could contact to ask for baby clothes and equipment, but she'd let her mother come up with ideas herself.

Nancy sniffed. Not a sign of disapproval of Lissa, more disapproval of the situation. 'What does she need? Does she have anything yet for the baby?'

'She has a few clothes from a charity shop, some onesies and singlets. And some bassinet sheets and blanket. She's also got a baby sling. But no cot or change table or anything because she hasn't got anywhere to live.' Or anyway to carry them.

Nancy reached for the notepad and pen she used for shopping lists and turned to a blank page. 'She'll need more clothes and bedding.' The list began. 'And a pram. Jeanie and I are going in to Birraga this morning. We'll see if the Salvation Army shop can help. Beth's youngest girl is three now. She might have baby things left over. Who else can I ask?'

'Chloe and Paul?' Angie suggested. 'Andrew and Erin?'

Her mother tapped the pen against her chin, thinking. 'They've got mostly boys. And they're older. Not many babies and toddlers in town these days.'

Angie pottered around making a bowl of cereal for herself and let the accusatory glance pass without comment. Most of her contemporaries – not that there were many – had left town. Not much work or reason to stay and raise families.

Nancy continued with her thinking aloud and making her list, and Angie offered a suggestion every now and then while she ate her breakfast. Typical kitchen-table problem-solving.

It continued around a table in the bistro at the pub half an hour later, with her mother's good friend Jeanie Menotti after she finished her breakfast shift in the pub's kitchen. Fortunately for Angie's fatigue, that conversation also involved a mug of coffee, made by Jeanie, who didn't stint on the strength.

Nancy's list now covered a page and a half.

'The main issue, though,' Angie ventured, 'is somewhere for her to stay. Would you mind if she stayed at the pub, Mum? Just for a week or so over the holidays?'

'It's no place for a baby. Or a young girl,' Nancy

objected, as if the current guests were a rougher lot than Gil Gillespie, and Owen and his grandfather.

'There are a dozen vacant houses in town,' Jeanie mused, always practical. 'But apart from the fact they'd need to be cleaned and set up, she'll probably be better off staying at first with someone who has some experience with babies. And not having to manage everything herself.'

Her mother had experience raising babies and a spare room, even with Angie and her brother home for the week. But that might be too much for her mother, who hadn't even met Lissa yet. And possibly not the best for Lissa, given Nancy's tendency to worry about every small thing.

'Why don't you call in and see her when you're in Birraga?' Angie suggested. 'You can ask her what she wants. She will have probably seen the social worker, too, by the time you get there.'

Her phone buzzed and she excused herself to take the call. Megan, phoning in response to the text she'd sent a little earlier.

'Lissa's in *Birraga?*' Megan said the moment she answered. 'With a *baby?*'

'Yes. A little girl, born around midnight.'

'I have to go and see her. Are you there now?'

'No, I'm at the pub. My Mum and Jeanie are going in to Birraga soon. They'll probably be able to give you a lift.'

'Yes please, if they can. I've been so worried about her. I'll be there in ten minutes.'

She made it to the pub in eight minutes, breathing heavily after rushing from her grandmother's home.

Not much past seventeen, she'd toned down the goth look since she'd arrived in Dungirri six months earlier, but she still kept the ear and nose studs. In the long months Angie had tried to keep the pub afloat after her father's death, she'd come to know Megan, and she admired the way the girl had done her best to make the relationship with her elderly natural grandparents work. Angie returned her affectionate hug but had little time to answer questions as Jeanie and Nancy were almost ready to leave.

'Are you coming with us, Angela?' her mother asked.

'No, I'll go and see her this afternoon. And do any last minute shopping if you've forgotten anything.' Birraga would be pretty much shut down by four o'clock on Christmas Eve, and wouldn't open again for a few days.

After they'd left, she briefly contemplated and then dismissed the idea of seeing if Owen was awake. He needed some more sleep. So did she. And she would likely see him this afternoon.

As she walked the short distance back to her mother's home, the rising wind blew her hair around her face and she had to hold it back to keep it out of her eyes. One particularly strong gust almost pushed the front door out of her hand, and she had to push to close it.

She doubted she'd actually get much sleep at this hour of the morning, but she kicked off her sandals and lay down on the bed anyway. After ten minutes her thoughts still raced. She reached for her phone, and for the first time since yesterday morning she checked her work emails. Just in case there'd been a response to the report she'd given her boss two days ago.

Only one new email in her inbox, from the company's admin manager, with the subject, *Official notification*. Official notification of what? The email loaded painfully slowly. *Dear Ms Butler, I regret to inform you that due to a restructure within the company, your position has become redundant, effective immediately.*

She bolted upright, sitting on the edge of the bed as she skimmed the paragraphs about payment of entitlements and collection of personal belongings.

It didn't start to sink in until she re-read that opening line . . . *your position has become redundant, effective immediately.*

~

'A detective?' Owen eyed the closed door of the room in the ward that they'd moved his grandfather in to earlier in the day. 'Why does a detective want to speak with him? He didn't really see the aggressive guy last night.'

The young student nurse shook her head, 'No, it's not about that. He asked us to call the detective in. So we did. And then he asked not to be disturbed. That was over half an hour ago. You could wait in the foyer. They probably won't be much longer.'

Or he could knock and go in and find out . . . Although tempted, he decided against it out of respect for his grandfather's wishes. The foyer at the entrance to the ward contained a few armchairs, some magazines on the coffee table, and a bookshelf in the corner. The magazines were the celebrity gossip type, of no interest to him, so he found himself standing in front of the bookshelf. It took some moments for his continually racing thoughts to focus on the books. All used, and an assortment of titles. He wasn't sure he actually wanted to read anything.

The name "O'Connell" leapt out at him from the spine of one of the books. Patrick O'Connell. A collection of short stories. He pulled it from the shelf, and idly flicked through it. Angie had mentioned that Delphi's brother was an author, and sure enough, the biography said he was a local man originally.

But when he turned to the back cover, the sight of the author photo snatched his breath away.

Apart from some grey on Patrick's temples, he could have been looking at a photo of himself.

CHAPTER 5

The detective who emerged from his grandfather's room was about his own age, with a firm handshake and easy manner as he introduced himself to Owen.

'I'm Steve Fraser. I've heard you had a busy night last night. Thanks for assisting my colleagues.'

Owen brushed off the thanks. With no one else in the vicinity to overhear, he asked straight out, 'I understand my grandfather asked to see you. Why?'

'You'll have to discuss it with him, I'm afraid. Privacy and all that. But can I ask *you* – your grandfather seems mentally with it. He is, isn't he? In sound mind, as they say?'

'Yes.'

'Knows truth from reality? Not inclined to imagine things that didn't happen? Or make up stories to gain attention?'

The idea was so ridiculous Owen struggled to keep a biting edge from his reply. 'Absolutely not, Detective. He's far saner and more grounded than most people.'

Fraser nodded with a grimace. 'Yeah. That's what I was afraid of.' He took a business card from his pocket. 'Call me if you need to. I have to go research some laws, and statutes of limitation.'

Another hazy suspicion added to the half-formed ones already circling in Owen's thoughts. 'Has my grandfather confessed to some type of crime?'

'He's made an admission,' Fraser conceded. 'I have yet to determine whether a crime has been committed.'

'He's never had so much as a speeding ticket or a parking ticket.' Not the smartest thing to say, but on top of everything else he could scarcely grapple with the idea that his grandfather obviously believed he'd done something against the law.

'Yeah, well, I'll be in touch. Thanks for your time.' He shook hands again before briskly striding away.

Owen needed a few minutes of space to think before he went in to see his grandfather. The foyer opened on to a garden, but the wind blew in strong gusts, hot and dry. He went instead to the kiosk and bought an apple juice, hoping the chilled liquid might clear his thoughts.

He stared through the window at the rose bushes swaying in the gusts as he drank the juice. What did he know? He looked like Delphi O'Connell's brother. His grandfather had known Delphi a long time ago. Delphi remembered him, but was more interested in Owen's mother.

He also knew his grandfather had been a loving and devoted father to his only daughter, despite the challenges of being a single father in the 1950s and

60s, after his wife deserted her husband and child.

Any number of scenarios could fit those facts. For one short moment, he considered the possibility that Delphi was his grandfather's errant wife. No. *'She may not remember me,'* he'd said. *'She may not know the wrong I did her.'* And the name Bernard had provided for the parental details on his mother's death certificate wasn't Philadelphia, although it was something equally unusual. Anastacia. A name mentioned only rarely in Owen's childhood, her absence decades long.

Why go over and over it all, searching for answers, when his grandfather had them?

They'd given Bernard a private room, although in a hospital this small there couldn't be many of them. He sat supported by pillows in a large armchair by the window, the tube for the oxygen trailing across the bed, the face mask replaced by nasal prongs.

'Back so soon?' His grandfather said, his voice weak. 'You should have got some rest.'

Owen pulled the visitor's chair closer and sat down, taking his grandfather's hand. Nowhere near as puffy as last night. A good sign. But his eyes were red-rimmed, and he seemed weary. Perhaps from a broken night, or from his illness, or perhaps his discussion with the detective had tired him.

'I visited Delphi O'Connell,' he began, and watched for his grandfather's reaction, in case he was too tired to talk. 'She accepted the briefcase, asked after my mother, and told me to come back after lunch.'

'Ah.' He fiddled with the oxygen tube, and said

nothing else.

'Granddad, I've got some pieces of the jigsaw but I haven't got enough to fit them together yet. The detective clearly knows more than I do but he wouldn't tell me. You don't have to do it now, but when you're up to it, I'd like you to tell me what you told him. I can't help you if I don't know the full story.'

His grandfather clenched his hand tightly, and breathed several rapid breaths in, out, in, out, his face draining of colour. 'I told him . . . that about sixty years ago, I stole a baby.'

~

Angie ranted and swore, yelled and sobbed, allowing her emotions free-rein because she had the house to herself for now and no-one could witness her meltdown.

Bastards for doing this to her. Cowards for sending an email rather than the courtesy of a phone call, at the very least. As for the timing – Christmas Eve – oh, that smacked of her vindictive, arrogant, misogynistic boss. Yes, they'd all known that business was falling and finances tightening, and there'd been hints of a restructure, but this fast and this brutal? Totally unexpected.

She used up all of her mother's tissues and had to resort to toilet paper to wipe away tears and blow her nose. Harsh toilet paper that scratched because her mother economised in most things.

One more reason to stop crying and pull herself

together. If she could stop crying. Damn, this hurt.

'It's just a job,' she said aloud, as if hearing the words might convince her. 'Just a frigging job.' With work she loved and a good salary and some okay colleagues and the psychopathic boss from hell.

Maybe she should have put in a formal complaint about him. Maybe then they'd have made him redundant, instead of her.

No. Last on, first off. She'd only been there eighteen months, and she'd taken the grudgingly-given three months of leave without pay after her father died. Other than the fact she'd worked damned hard for the company, they didn't owe her a lot of loyalty.

Time to just deal with it. She brought her laptop to the kitchen table, made a cup of tea, and with a roll of toilet paper beside her, sat down to read through the email again. Her salt-drenched eyes stung as she read the attached documents on the screen, but the personal hurt and some of the anger dissipated when she studied the revised organisational chart and realised that most of her section had been absorbed into another one and that her boss's position had been made redundant, too. Maybe he'd received an email this morning as well. Or maybe they'd put him somewhere else in the company.

It should no longer matter to her. Perhaps in time it wouldn't.

They were giving her two months' pay as a termination payment, a little more than her contract provided for because of the Christmas holiday timing. Kinda generous of them, except for the whole redundancy at Christmas nightmare they'd inflicted on her.

She should start making a list of what she needed to do. Update her CV. Search the employment sites. Make a list of companies to approach. Work out a budget to see how long her savings and two months' pay could last her.

She sat with her pen poised on her mother's notepad but she couldn't bring herself to start writing. Her gut churned and her eyes leaked again and her thoughts swirled in an incessant whirlpool of fears and insecurities and worries.

Thinking clearly right now? Not going to happen. She drained her tea and shoved her chair back. She didn't have to solve everything straight away. She needed to get out, walk, get some air, find some chocolate or coffee or salty chips or some comfort food because alcohol wasn't a good idea at this hour of the day.

Her phone beeped with a message. A photo from Megan, a smiling selfie of her and Lissa with the bundled-up baby between them, not much more visible than a fuzz of dark hair and closed eyes above the tiny nose.

The happy photo made her smile, and also helped to put her problems into perspective. She had family, a home with her mother if she needed it, and savings, skills, and experience. Things might not be easy for a while, but she'd be okay.

Feeling more resolute, she splashed her red eyes with cool water and braided her hair before she ventured out, but the hot wind whipped her face, harsh with heat and dust. And the slight scent of smoke. She instinctively looked north, searching for evidence of a fire. The Dungirri Scrub bordered the town to the east and north, stretching for tens of kilometres of dry forest. A thin column of white rose above the tree-line in the distance into the clear blue sky.

The siren at the Rural Fire Service shed on the edge of town burst in to its warning wail, and before she'd made it to the pub, at least six people had hurried out, leapt into cars, and driven the two blocks down to the shed.

Eleni and George Pappas came out of their general store opposite the pub to stand on the corner, watching to the north. Angie crossed the road to join them as another couple of vehicles passed on their way to the shed.

'It might be a flare-up from the fire a few days ago,' George informed her. 'It's still a fair distance from town.'

'Bad day for it, though.' She didn't elaborate. George and Eleni knew the dangers as well as she did. If the fire caught in the tree tops the wind would blow burning leaves for miles, starting spot fires.

Eleni kissed her on the cheek and although she gave her a searching stare, and squeezed her arm gently, she didn't comment on her probably still red eyes. Perceptive, as always. When Angie and her brother Dave hadn't been hanging around the pub as kids, they'd been over here at the shop, out the back with Lexi Pappas and her older brother Andrew. Or roaming the Dungirri streets with them, biking up to the waterhole, fishing for yabbies in the creek. The shop was never as busy as the pub, so Eleni had patched up her grazed knees and applied ointment to insect bites and wiped up tears from injuries and upsets. It didn't seem so many years ago, but now Andrew was an accountant, married to a vet, and Lexi taught high school in Birraga.

An SUV came down the street and pulled in beside them. Lexi in her RFS uniform, and three young kids. Andrew's family. Dungirri school kids still recovering from injuries from the bus accident.

Eleni and George helped the kids out, and Angie went to the back of the vehicle to assist Lexi with a wheelchair.

'School holidays,' Lexi said in explanation. 'I've been minding the sproggets this week while Andrew and Erin are working.' She nodded back towards the smoke. 'But it's all hands on deck for this one.'

Lexi drove off with a wave as soon as the kids were unloaded. George and Eleni shepherded their grandchildren into the cool inside.

Angie crossed the road to the pub. All hands on deck. Communities like Dungirri ran on volunteers, and everyone did what they could in emergencies. She'd left town at eighteen, never joined or trained with the RFS or SES, but if this fire turned bad there'd surely be something, somewhere, that she could do. Even if it was making sandwiches for the emergency services.

Funny how she still thought of herself as part of the community, although she'd left more than ten years ago and only come home for a week or two a year until her Dad died. And funny how some part of her brain still obstinately labelled it 'home'.

Her phone buzzed as she pushed open the gate into the pub's courtyard.

'It's your Mum here,' Nancy said when she answered.

Yes, Mum, I knew that. My phone tells me. 'What's up, Mum?'

'I'm still in Birraga. But Jeanie's frantic with worry. You need to go out to Delphi's place and make sure she's alright. You need to go now. She's not answered her phone for hours.'

'She's probably just doing some work on the farm, Mum. You know phone reception's not great out there.' But despite her reassurances, Angie turned a one-eighty and headed back out through the gate. Delphi must be past seventy. Tough as boot leather and fiercely independent, but yeah, not young anymore.

'She received some news today. That man, Owen, he went and saw her this morning. He might have distressed her a great deal. Jeanie's worried that she might have . . .' Nancy didn't finish the sentence.

Owen distress *Delphi?* Aside from the unlikelihood of Owen upsetting anyone, Delphi rarely gave a blue fig what anyone thought. Yet Owen had mentioned his grandfather wanting him to do him a favour this morning, and he hadn't seemed happy about it. Not that she could imagine Doctor Chynoweth, with his old-world gentlemanly courtesy, distressing anyone, either.

But an elderly woman alone on a farm, not

answering her phone . . . 'I'll just grab some gear and go right out there,' Angie told her mother.

~

'I stole a baby . . .'

The words tumbled around and around in Owen's mind but he asked no more questions. When his grandfather's oxygen levels rose a little and his breathing became somewhat easier, Owen and the nurse assisted him back into bed. Once the nurse had recorded the routine observations and left, Bernard gripped Owen's hand again and insisted on telling his story. It came slowly, in whispers and sentence fragments, the telling painful both emotionally and physically.

The late 1950s, and a small town in rural Queensland. His wife was pregnant, the first pregnancy she'd carried to term after three miscarriages. A nervous breakdown – that's what they'd called it then – after the third miscarriage, with episodes of mania and self-harm, threats of suicide.

'I was at a loss,' Bernard said. 'We did not know then what we know now, about mental health. Treatments were drastic, and I would not let her be committed. But as the due date for the baby came closer, she seemed better, making plans for it, sewing and setting up the nursery. I believed – I truly believed – that having the baby to care for and love would save her.'

Owen held back the questions about the

grandmother who had ultimately deserted her husband and child. He let his grandfather talk uninterrupted, although he kept an eye on the screen that monitored his heartbeat.

Bernard told how as a small-town doctor his patients included the residents in the Church-run home where unmarried girls were sent by their families to hide their pregnancies. A strict institution, as if the girls were to blame for their predicament, for being 'loose'. Young unmarried women often faced the threat of being disowned by their families, with little recourse to employment, financial support, or child care, and were under immense pressure to relinquish their newborns for adoption.

'Philadelphia . . . ' he said, 'She kept to herself, worked hard. She was very pragmatic about surrendering her child when it was born. Her father would disown her if she kept the baby . . . She knew it would not be possible for a girl of seventeen, without family or community, to raise a child alone.'

Owen found it hard to imagine the woman he'd met this morning as a teenager. Except perhaps he could. Photos of his mother in her youth showed that same strong face, not fine enough features to be classically beautiful, but alive with spirit and determination and attractive for that.

'My wife and Philadelphia were in labour on the same night. The midwife from the home, Sister Kendall, had brought Philadelphia in to the hospital, and she assisted me. But my wife . . . her labour was long, and difficult.'

The memories were becoming stressful for his

grandfather, but he waved away Owen's suggestion to stop for now. 'You must know this. When the baby came . . . she had no heartbeat and she didn't breathe. I couldn't get her to breathe.' He closed his eyes, his hand clutching the sheet. 'I carried her tiny body out of the delivery room . . . ' His voice shook and cracked. 'My daughter. I tried and tried, and Sister Kendall tried, and we could not save her. I could not save my daughter.'

Tears ran down his face, the grief bottled up for so long still raw and deep. Owen had an inkling of what was to come, and suspected that this might be the first time that Bernard had ever shared his devastating sorrow. Owen reached for the tissue box and offered it.

'I'm so sorry, Granddad. That must have been heart-breaking. Take your time. You don't have to tell me all this now.'

'I do.' But his grandfather blew his nose and wiped his eyes, and breathed deeply of the oxygen while he fought to compose himself again.

'Philadelphia delivered her baby, just minutes later. A healthy little girl. The practice then – it was thought kinder for the relinquishing mother – was to take the baby immediately. So that they didn't form a bond that would be harder to break. Sister Kendall took the child from the room. I followed her . . . I was barely coping, and dreading breaking the news to my wife. I feared for her sanity and her life.'

Another long pause as he struggled for enough breath. 'When Sister checked the baby and wrapped her up, she . . . ' He hesitated, before he finished his confession in a rush, 'She put the healthy child in my arms . . . and told me to take my daughter to my wife. And I did. I could never tell her. I feared it would break her if she knew.'

Suspicions and jigsaw puzzle pieces fell into place, and Owen struggled to determine his thoughts about his grandfather's revelations. At one level he could grasp that the immense emotion of going straight from losing one's own child to the birth of a healthy one, wailing with easy breaths, would undermine reasoning.

A moment's decision in grief, and a life-long secret that could not be told. Or could it have been? Did the protection of an innocent party – a mentally fragile woman – justify the continued lie? Did the social conditions and knowledge of half a century ago mitigate the decision? He didn't know. He couldn't work his way through the complexities, separate logic and emotion.

'Did your wife suspect? Is that why she left?'

Bernard shook his head. 'She never neglected your mother. . . but she did not warm to motherhood. She was restless, always restless. When my sister came from England to visit . . . Anastacia went to Brisbane for a short break.'

And never came back. Owen knew the basics of the history from there. His mother, Marion, raised by her father and her Aunt Sophia, who married and lived nearby. Anastacia's continued absence, her relationship with another man. Marion had never really known her, had accepted, at least as an adult, that some women were not natural mothers. And she had never been short of love.

'Why didn't you divorce your wife?' he asked. Even before the no-fault divorce laws of the 1970s, Bernard could have divorced her for desertion, or adultery. But he regretted the question when his grandfather rested his head back against the pillow, clearly tiring.

'Wedding vows,' Bernard murmured in answer. 'Responsible . . . In sickness and in health. Before God. She never asked . . . for divorce. She still had some episodes . . . of instability. Her partner cared for her. But not well.'

His wedding vows. Owen began to comprehend a little more of *why*. Why the secrecy, why for so long. How, for Bernard, honouring his wedding vows had outweighed the other competing demands on his honour.

'She's not still alive, is she? Anastacia?'

Another weak shake of Bernard's head. 'August . . . she died.'

In August. And here was Bernard, in December, revealing the long-held secret, making himself accountable by confessing to Delphi and to the police.

His grandfather gripped his hand tightly again. 'Can't give Philadelphia . . . her daughter. Only memories. Memories, and photos . . . and you.'

He closed his eyes, breathed out on a sigh, and his clasp loosened. For an instant, Owen's own heart faltered in fear. But his grandfather drew breath again, evenly in and out, and his pulse rate steadied.

The relief of laying down a heavy burden, perhaps.

Or of passing it to stronger shoulders. His shoulders. Just as he'd taken up the responsibility for his sister and brother after their mother died, now he had to accept responsibility for navigating the situation, the relationship, with Delphi. His grandmother. If she wanted a relationship.

'Your mother – was she happy?' The longing in the words, the years of not knowing . . . Delphi might not want a relationship, not an acknowledged one, but she might crave more, more information perhaps than the memories and photographs in his grandfather's briefcase. Given his grandfather's frailty, he would have to carry that duty for him.

He stayed with his grandfather a little while longer, mostly in silence to allow him rest, sometimes a word here and there as he offered him some water, rearranged his pillows. He stayed to assure himself that Bernard was not about to slip away, that revealing the truth had not stressed his heart too much.

When the kitchen lady brought lunch around, Owen rose to his feet and moved towards the door while she set up the tray. 'I'd better go, Granddad. I'll go back and see her now.'

'Thank you, Owen. I hope one day . . . you will forgive me. For betraying your trust in me.'

Owen returned to the bedside and waited until they were alone again. 'Granddad, it was a different time, and you only thought of others. Your whole life, you've put others before yourself. I've always loved and respected you. Nothing changes that.'

He hugged his grandfather close, and as he left the room he dashed away some moisture from his eye.

Before he left the hospital he went in search of Lissa's room, in the other wing. A seventeen-year-old with a new-born baby. A teenager with no family support who had grown up in a welfare system still so far from perfect.

How much had really changed, in sixty years? Despite all the laws and regulations and policies, the protection of children still relied, ultimately, on those who cared for them having the decency, compassion, and the commitment to love and nurture them.

What would his mother's fate have been if she'd gone through the adoption process? A period in a babies' home perhaps – and there were nightmare stories about some of those emerging now – before placement with an adopting couple. Despite the vetting of those wishing to adopt, there were no guarantees. No guarantees then, and no guarantees now.

At least Lissa had the choice to keep her baby. Unlike Delphi.

But the hard truth remained that with no official register of an adoption, his grandfather's actions had denied his mother the chance to meet her natural mother, and denied Delphi the chance to know her daughter.

When he knocked on the door of Lissa's room he found her dressed and in an armchair, the baby contentedly asleep in her arms. Her friend Megan – the teenager from the pub, Gillespie's daughter – sat with her, the two of them deep in adoration of the baby.

Lissa greeted him with a shy smile. 'Doctor Morag said we can be discharged tomorrow. I'm going to stay with Megan and her Grandma for a little while. I'm very lucky, very grateful to them.'

'Grandma was a mothercraft nurse,' Megan added. 'She knows about babies. She said it was a long time ago, but that babies haven't changed.'

Some of the theories might have changed, but Owen kept that thought to himself. The calm and experience of a mothercraft nurse would be a good support for Lissa as she learned to care for her child. 'I'm glad you have things sorted out. All the best, Lissa. She's a beautiful little girl.'

In the carpark Angie's mother Nancy and Jeanie unloaded several shopping bags from the car, although Jeanie had her phone to her ear, her face creased with concern. She signalled him to stop when she saw him. 'Could you go and check the woolshed, Angie?' she said into the phone. 'And see if the quad bike is in the machinery shed? Hold on a minute – Owen's here.' She didn't lower the phone as she asked him, 'How was Delphi when you left her, Owen? Did she say anything about where she was going? She hasn't answered her phone for hours.'

Delphi missing. He tried to recall what she'd said earlier. 'She said she had to fix some fencing.' Would that take hours? He had no clue. 'But she was a bit shaken. I didn't understand why, then. Now I do. I'm on my way back there.'

'Good. I'll go with you.' She spoke directly into the phone again as she passed her car keys to Nancy, 'Angie, we'll be there soon. Your Mum can bring my car later, when she's finished here. If you can check the sheds and the garden, we'll meet you at the house in half an hour or so.'

Half an hour for fifty-five kilometres? Mostly long straight road, so doable. Jeanie buckled herself into his passenger seat quickly, urgency holding her tense. Her concern for her friend made him more worried, too. All going well, Angie would have found her by the time they arrived. But if not . . . With the wind and the heat and the dust, it wasn't a good day for an older woman to be missing.

As he turned on to the main road, Jeanie said frankly, without beating around the bush, 'I know that Delphi gave up a baby for adoption, when she was very young, And you're the image of her brother, Patrick. I knew him well. I can put two and two together, so you'd better tell me the rest. You and Delphi can trust my discretion. I've known her for more than fifty years.'

He hoped he *could* trust her discretion, because as the kilometres sped by, he outlined the history. Delphi might never want it publicly known that she'd borne a child, and he understood and respected that.

He didn't exceed the speed limit often because the wind still blew strongly, dust swirled in the air, and every kilometre or so leaf debris or tree branches littered the road. At one point an SES crew worked to clear a fallen tree, its huge trunk straddling the road with debris spread over a large area from the impact of its fall. They'd cleared a narrow track, and Owen had to edge through it, slowly and carefully.

Jeanie made few comments and asked only a

couple of questions as he related what Bernard had told him. He didn't gloss over or gild his grandfather's actions. He doubted Bernard would want him to.

Some of his unease must have shown, because when he finished Jeanie said gently, 'Don't judge him too harshly, Owen. Those were different times, different understandings of adoption. We know how problematic it can be now, but back then, many adopted children were never told of their origin by their adoptive parents. And for mothers giving up their babies, it was expected to be forever. Reunions only became possible in the 1970s.'

'Mum was never adopted,' he pointed out. 'She was registered at birth as their child.'

'That and similar things happened a lot more than you might think. Even in small communities.'

Something in her tone made him think that she held some of those secrets. A compassionate woman, grounded in good sense – yes, she would be the type of woman others confided in.

She'd checked her phone frequently, holding it to the window for reception for much of the trip.

'Have you always worked at the pub?' he asked, in an attempt to distract her from worrying.

'No. I had the service station and café until recently, but a fire destroyed it.'

Which must be why she was staying with Delphi. 'That cleared block across the road from the pub? Was that it?'

'Yes. I'm a little old to start all over again, but we're working on a plan to rebuild it. The town needs a fuel station.'

Owen glanced at his fuel gauge. He'd have to remember to fill up next time he drove to Birraga.

A fire tanker overtook him as smoke mixed with the dust haze, tinging the air an orange brown against the blue of the sky. A burning leaf blew against his windscreen.

'There's a fire to the north,' Jeanie said. 'They'll have a hard time controlling it today. I'll go down to the RFS shed just as soon as we know Delphi's okay.' She pointed towards a gate up ahead. 'That's her place there.'

Angie's ute was over in the working area by the garage, next to Delphi's. She came around from the back as he pulled up in front of the house, her hair tucked up under a broad-brimmed hat, a cotton work shirt over moleskins and boots.

'No sign of her yet,' Angie told them. 'Her quad bike's gone, so she could be anywhere on the place.'

Owen looked out over the paddocks, the pockets of forest here and there, the low hills to the east and south, the snaking line of trees in the distance, and the glint of a dam. 'How large is her property?'

'Four thousand hectares,' Jeanie replied. 'Ten thousand acres.'

Neither measurement helped him envision the area, but they had to mean a few kilometres. Not a small place.

Movement caught his eye, in grass down beyond the garage. 'What's that?' he asked. An animal, jerky in its motion. A dog, limping heavily.

Angie set off towards it, and he followed.

Delphi's cattle dog. Angie dropped to her knee

and it approached her cautiously. Owen held back a little so as not to scare it.

'He's hurt,' she said over her shoulder to him, as she carefully felt over the dog. It flinched and growled when she touched the hip, but permitted the examination, and even from a couple of metres away Owen saw the bleeding lacerations on its side.

Angie's face held nothing of her usual lightness when she turned to him. 'We'll have to take him up to the house then go and look for Delphi. If the dog's this badly hurt, chances are she's hurt, somewhere, too.'

CHAPTER 6

The dog bared its teeth at Owen, so Angie carried it up to the house, mostly avoiding smearing blood on her shirt. The wind worried her. The heat worried her. And the damned fire worried the hell out of her. She'd already stamped out one lot of burning embers that had dropped from the sky. And Delphi was out there somewhere, probably injured.

'I'll look after the dog,' Jeanie assured her as she laid him carefully on his blanket on the veranda beside the door. 'We'll get him to the vet later. I'm going to phone the SES and call in their help in the search. And – ' She too, glanced over her shoulder to the increasing cloud of smoke to the north. 'I'll get the pump going to fill the spare water tank and get the fire-fighting trailer out. Just in case.'

Trust Jeanie to be so practical and level-headed, despite her fears.

'Good. If Delphi said she had to fix a fence,' Angie said, 'Then we'll start at the creek. I've got a radio in the ute, Jeanie, so I can keep in touch with

SES with that. You okay to come with me, Owen?' She hoped they wouldn't need his skills, and feared that they would. At least he was adequately dressed for bush bashing at the creek. Jeans, boots, shirt. She had a spare hat in her ute.

Owen didn't hesitate. 'I'm coming. Do you have a first aid kit?'

'Basic. Blanket, dressings, snake bandage, antiseptic,' she explained while they crossed to her vehicle. 'But I do have a sat phone as well as the radio.' So they could call in help, if necessary. Assuming they found her.

'Why the creek?' he asked as she reversed the ute just far enough to swing around Delphi's and head down a farm track across the paddock.

'A likely place to have fence damage. Water damage after heavy rain. Stock or feral animal damage in the dry, when they're trying to reach water.'

'I never asked you what you do. You're obviously familiar with farming.'

She shifted into low-range gear as she turned off the main track to follow wheel paths in the dry grass along a fence line towards the creek.

'Not so much farming. I did environmental science at uni. I work . . . *worked* in an environmental consultancy.' Her eyes were welling again and the ground was too rough for her to take her hands from the steering wheel. A tear slid down her cheek. Dammit, she'd have to explain. Preferably without cracking up. Definitely without looking at him because sympathy might just undo her shaky control. 'Redundancy notice in my email this morning.

Effective immediately.'

'Shit. That sucks. It's frigging callous timing to do that to you.'

Even his mild swearing sounded sympathetic.

'Yeah.' She choked out the single word.

'If you need to drown your sorrows later, I'll buy the drinks.'

She gave a strangled laugh. 'And scrape me off the ground when I fall down after the second one? I don't drink much.'

Warmth mellowed his voice. 'If necessary. And see you safely to your door.'

Of course he would. He was that kind of rare man who put others' needs first. He'd probably even hold back her hair while she threw up into the toilet.

Except she didn't plan on consuming anything stronger than coffee. Okay, and her mother's Christmas cake. There might well be a good dose of medicinal brandy in that. Her mother's dislike of alcohol had a blind spot when it came to Christmas baking.

She dragged her thoughts back to the task ahead of them. Delphi, and what might have happened. 'Jeanie said you saw Delphi this morning. That you might have told her something upsetting.'

'Yes.' He took a long moment before he continued. 'Granddad met her a long time ago, in difficult circumstances. He asked me to give her some information, related to that.'

And there was a very careful, enigmatic answer. A quick glance across at him showed his face serious, thoughtful. 'You're not going to explain any more, are you?'

'I'm sorry. It's not for me to share.'

Confidential, upsetting news. Despite her curiosity, she didn't probe further. Delphi had always kept herself to herself and deserved that respect.

The fence line began to dip down towards the creek, and she stopped the ute in full sun, well away from the old red gums along the creek banks that could drop deadly branches even when there was no wind. She almost wished she had a hard hat with her, although even a hard hat would be little protection against a falling chunk of timber.

She retrieved her day pack from the back seat, holding the standard safety equipment she carried when working in the field. GPS, sat phone, snake bandage, water bottles. She hadn't charged any batteries for a few days but they should still be fine for an emergency. Her mobile phone had no signal, useless.

She tossed a tube of sunscreen and a company cap to Owen. Not a decent hat but it would shade his face and head. 'I've got a couple of litres of water. Just let me know when you want some.' No need to warn a doctor about dehydration.

'Thanks.' He slathered sunscreen on to the back of his neck. No need to warn him about sunburn, either. She liked sensible men.

From the tracks in the grass, she was fairly certain the quad bike had come this way at some time, but maybe not today. In this heat, there was no natural spring in the native grasses to bounce back after pressure. And she couldn't see the quad from here.

'If we can cross the creek, we'll follow the fence up to the top of that rise,' she told Owen. 'We should have a reasonable view from there.'

The creek banks were high and wide, carved by a millennia of occasional floods after heavy rain, exposing the twisted roots of the river gums that stretched, metres long, down into the water table. Yet the creek bed itself was sandy and dry, with only a few puddles of stagnant water here and there.

Where the fence crossed the creek the bank wasn't quite so steep, and they followed the fence line on foot. They saw no quad bike tracks or boot prints as they crossed the deep sand of the creek bed. Delphi hadn't been here today.

The wind and sun made the walk up the exposed rise beyond the creek uncomfortably hot, although it wasn't particularly steep. But as the highest point in the vicinity the rise offered an almost three-sixty-degree view over the surrounding landscape.

Angie passed a bottle of water to Owen when they reached the top, and glugged down a few mouthfuls from her own. The dust haze cloaked the horizon, darker to the north where the bushfire smoke thickened it. Even with her binoculars, she could barely see the scrub beyond Dungirri, five kilometres away.

'Most of what you can see used to be O'Connell property,' she told Owen. 'East as far as Geary's Road, on the edge of Dungirri. And west – oh, a fair few kilometres. Some of it was carved up in the early 1900s, with the Closer Settlement Acts. But see where the light is glinting off the roof over there?

That's Johnno Dawson's place. Delphi sold that portion of land to his father in the 1960s, after her father died.'

She looked to see if she was boring him and found him studying her, his mouth quirking into a smile. 'You love history, don't you?'

'I find it fascinating,' she confessed. 'How the land has been used, shaped, changed. Where the water flows, what the soil is like, what grows where. Not just crops, but native vegetation, food for wildlife and birds.' She caught herself and stopped before she launched into a full-scale environment lecture.

'But water's the most important, isn't it?' he mused. 'And competition for it can become the source of conflict.'

He'd worked in Syria and presumably other areas of conflict, and she knew how drought and water access could become a key driver of division and civil war. She'd love to hear his views and experience.

'Absolutely. But we'd better save the geopolitics for later, over a nice cold drink, after we've found Delphi.' She raised the binoculars to her eyes again and followed the line of the creek, meandering through the paddocks. No sign of a quad bike, or Delphi. But trees often obscured the view – trees along the creek, and the corridors of trees Delphi had planted over the years bordering paddocks and providing shade and refuge to stock and wildlife.

Owen shaded his eyes with his hand and searched, too. 'I don't see any stock. Has it been too dry?'

'Apparently she sold the last lot off this week. She's getting ready to sell the place. Shame to see it leave the family, but there's only Bella, her niece, and her life is elsewhere. Although Jeanie said Bella and Alec are arriving later today, for Christmas.'

And Angie hoped there would not be bad news to meet them. She contemplated the path of the creek again. 'Let's try the creek at that paddock there, where it takes the bend. That's probably where she's had stock most recently – it's eaten down. We'll have to go back to the ute and drive around, though.'

The temperature was still climbing, but she drank no more of her water. Delphi might need it. If they found her.

'You mentioned Delphi's niece,' Owen said as she drove on the rough track across the paddocks. 'Do you know her?'

'Bella? Yes. But not well. She's a few years older than me, and she and her father left Dungirri years ago, when she was still in high school. She became a detective.' Angie didn't go in to recent history, and Bella's involvement with an investigation in Dungirri. Too complicated. 'Her partner is a police inspector,' she finished. And if they hadn't found Delphi by the time Alec arrived, he'd have the connections to get resources for a full-scale search.

He was silent as she turned off the track to follow a fence line to the creek. But a hundred metres down she caught a glint of something through the tress. Maybe water? Maybe . . . she resisted the urge to speed over the rough ground. Not much grass here, but she thought she could see faint wheel tracks.

She pulled up just before the trees. Ahead in the creek bed, a large one had toppled over, its root system tearing away from the bank and standing vertically now, two metres high.

'That blue there,' Owen said, already out the door. 'Is that . . . ?'

'Yes.' Angie grabbed her pack and the first aid kit from the back, her heart pounding. 'That's the quad, under the tree branches.'

~

Owen half-sprinted, half-slid down the bank of the creek by the fence but as he reached the sand the fallen tree created a twenty-metre-wide barricade, the top branches across the fence further on.

'This way,' Angie said, pushing the already bowed fence further down so they could scramble across. 'Watch the barbed wire. And keep an eye out for snakes.'

As they skirted around the tree and back through the wires on the far side of the creek bed, Owen was more concerned with looking for Delphi than snakes. The quad bike lay half-crushed on its side, mostly covered by the large branches and foliage of the top quarter of the tree. He had to scramble and clamber over metres of horizontal tree to reach it, and he dreaded what he'd find.

Angie wasn't far behind him, and as he got close to the quad she helped him pull away some of the smaller leafy branches for better access. The quad had a roll bar, he saw, and that still held one of the larger branches off the ground.

But he couldn't see Delphi.

He yanked some branches off to clear his view around the quad, and squeezed under the larger branch to crouch in the small space underneath it, created by the quad and the roll bar.

Angie asked, 'Is she . . .?'

His throat dry, he answered, 'She's not here. But she was. Or the dog was. There's blood and the sand is gouged up.'

Bent low, he searched for any sign that she'd tried to crawl out, under the branches. He found a handprint in the sand, and a boot print, not his. And then he saw what he hadn't seen when he'd been so focused on the quad. An area of broken branches, where she'd pushed and pulled herself up and over them.

Angie found her tracks in the soft sand of the creek bed, beyond the tree. A single line of boot prints, with a drag mark beside it. 'She's injured,' she said. 'But moving.'

He thought he had his directions right. 'Following the creek towards the homestead?'

'Yes. We're about three k's away.' She shrugged her pack off her shoulders. 'You take this and follow her. I'll go back to the ute and radio the SES. Jeanie called them — they shouldn't be too far away, if they're not caught up elsewhere with the fire or wind damage. I'll drive round to that first place we stopped, and work back along the creek to meet you.'

'Unless she's already gone past that point.'

'If I see her tracks, I'll know. Good luck!'

He settled the pack on his back, adjusted the straps and set off at a run. The soft sand of the creek bed made hard-going, though, and Delphi must have found the same thing, as her tracks moved to the edge of the sand, still soft, but not as deep. The added advantage of patches of shade from the trees made the going easier, too. Apart from some small pools of stagnant, algae-covered water, the creek was dry.

He saw signs where she'd stopped, twice, resting on long-fallen tree trunks. She had to be in considerable pain, and quite likely dehydrated. For a woman in her seventies, that would compound any other medical conditions. She'd been out here for several hours now. He should have asked Jeanie about her health and medications.

He found her about two kilometres down, slumped against a rock in a bend in the creek. From a distance, he feared the worst. She lay at an odd angle, unmoving, cuts and bruises on her face and arms, her eyes closed. But as he approached her eyes shot open and although she didn't shift her head she said, her voice rasping, 'Watch out for the snake.'

He stopped, mid-pace. 'Where is it?'

'Brown snake. Near my leg. Can't see if it's still there.'

Conscious and coherent – good. *Snake* . . . She gripped her leg with a white-knuckled hand and he could see what appeared to be a belt around it. 'Did it bite you?'

'No. Haven't moved in case it's still there.'

For how long? How long had she held rigid, unmoving, and in great pain? He dropped to one knee, looked carefully around her feet, her legs –

she'd crafted a rough splint from sticks on her lower left – and around where she lay. 'I can't see it, Delphi. It must have gone.'

She breathed out with a groan and he moved in to help support her as she struggled in to a more comfortable position. She flinched in pain and swore. 'Bloody leg. Think it's broken. I yanked the quad around when I heard the tree falling and it rolled. Probably saved me from the tree, though.'

He eyed the splint, but didn't touch it. Not yet. If it was broken – he guessed maybe a fractured fibula, since she'd made it this far – it might well be swollen and agonising to remove the splint to see her leg.

'Delphi, the good news is, I'm a doctor. But the bad news is, I don't have any pain killers with me. Angie and the SES will be here very soon and we'll get you some pain relief as soon as possible.'

'It's bearable. If I don't move.'

She was gutsy, all right. Wiry, fit despite her age, and strong-willed and determined enough to limp over a kilometre towards help with a leg fracture and countless contusions and lacerations.

He unscrewed the cap of the water bottle and gave it to her. A risk, giving her water, but she'd made it this far so he doubted she had major internal or head injuries, and therefore dehydration was the greater risk. If she had to have surgery on her leg or anywhere else, she'd need to be airlifted from Birraga and it would be hours away yet. 'Just drink a mouthful at a time.'

She took a large gulp, then eyed him over the top of the bottle. 'A doctor, huh? Like your-' She hesitated a fraction. '. . . grandfather.'

He hunted for the first aid kit in the bottom of Angie's pack. How did he ease into this subject? He should tell her he knew the truth. Or his grandfather's perspective on it, anyway. 'My mother trained in medicine, too, although she went into research rather than practice. She became a professor in immunology.'

'So he said. In his letter.' Her grey eyes watched him, as if she wasn't sure what to reveal to him. He'd said to her this morning he didn't know his grandfather's secret. Now they tiptoed around, second guessing each other.

He laid out a dressing pack, using the backpack as a table. He thought he could hear the sound of vehicles in the distance. Which left them not much time to say what they needed to say to each other in private. Talking might be more urgent than dabbing antiseptic on her abrasions. He leaned back on his heels to look her in the eye. 'I saw my grandfather again this morning, after I visited you. He told me the truth. His letter must have been a huge shock for you.'

She gave a slight shake of her head. 'He thought I didn't know. But I was always fairly sure what had happened. The moment I saw your face, I knew for certain.'

Some of the tension he'd held since Bernard's confession ebbed away. She hadn't believed her child dead all these decades. 'I saw a photo of your brother. That will be me, in another few years.'

'Yes. But your mouth is different.'

He could definitely hear the rumble of an engine coming closer, perhaps driving up the creek. 'I'm sorry that you never had the chance to know her. And that we didn't have you in our lives. I can understand if you don't want to publicly acknowledge the relationship, but I hope you'll let my brother and sister and me get to know you.'

He waited while she drank some more water and considered him thoughtfully. 'Anyone who knew Patrick will see him in you, and to hell with anyone who speculates about his fidelity to Ruth. I'm too old to care what anyone thinks of me. We're not in the damn nineteen-fifties, anymore. So the world can know, as far as I'm concerned. Just don't ever,' she dropped her voice to a hiss as the SES truck pulled up nearby, 'call me Granny. Delphi will do just fine.'

He gave her a thumbs up and a grin before he went to meet the truck. Karl drove it, and Beth swung down from the passenger side.

'Angie's called for an ambulance. It's on its way. So is she. What are Delphi's injuries?' Beth asked.

Owen provided a brief summary of what he'd been able to assess of Delphi's condition while they unloaded equipment. 'Do you have pain relief you can give her?' he asked.

"I'll need to check some medical history with her first. Depending on what meds she's on, we can give her methoxyflurane,' Beth said.

'That's great.' An effective analgesic for emergency situations, and self-administered so Delphi had control of her pain, but wouldn't be able to overdose on it.

Owen stood back and let Beth and Karl do the work they were trained and skilled in. He'd be there if needed, if complications arose, but this was their speciality and they were equipped for this kind of environment. Delphi knew and trusted them – at least as far as she trusted anyone – and she answered questions and tolerated their examination. Like Owen, they didn't touch her leg, yet. Beth explained to her how to breathe in the methoxyflurane through the whistle-like inhaler and as the pain-killer gradually took effect, Delphi became more relaxed and somewhat drowsy.

Angie arrived with the paramedics on foot, having left the ambulance in a nearby paddock. As they set straight to work, she joined him in the shade of a tree nearby and handed him a bottle of water.

'I got more from the house, and you look like you can do with it. How is Delphi?'

'Remarkably good, given the circumstances. Probable fracture of the fibula – that's the smaller of the lower leg bones. But otherwise no major injury. That's the pain killer making her dopey, not injury.' He hoped. He'd seen no indication of other problems developing, but he kept a close watch on her, nonetheless.

'That's a huge relief. My imagination kept coming up with far worse scenarios.'

Just like his. 'It might have been worse. But thanks to your search strategy, we found her before dehydration and heat stress really kicked in.' In an elderly woman, another couple of hours could easily have been fatal.

'I just guessed. Luckily, as it turns out.'

'Educated and intuitive reasoning, more like it,' he said.

She tried to shrug off his comment but the faint rise of colour on her cheeks betrayed her.

He drank some of the water she'd brought, blissfully cool and fresh. For the first time he noticed that the wind no longer blew as strongly.

'The wind's dropped,' he commented.

'Yes. Thankfully. And I heard on the radio that the fire is under control. It burned into a fire break they made last week. So we can all go home and relax, once they've taken Delphi. I plan to catch up on some sleep. You probably need to, too.'

Sleep seemed the best idea in the world, and the most unattainable just now. 'I'll have to go back in to Birraga, make sure she's okay.'

'Surely Morag's okay enough to handle it? Isn't she?'

'Yes. Although she should be taking a few days off. But that's not the main reason I want to go.'

'Which is?'

'The thing is . . . It's a long story, but as it turns out, Delphi is-' He was about to simply say "family" until he remembered her concern for Patrick's reputation. 'My grandmother.'

She stared at him as if he'd started raving. 'Delphi. Your grandmother.' She spoke flatly, and when he didn't correct her she added, 'You're not joking, are you?'

'No.' They were far enough away from the others not to be overheard. 'My mother was Delphi's biological daughter.'

'Wow.' She started thinking through the implications. 'Who was . . .? Sorry, none of my business, I guess.'

'I don't know who Mum's father was. There hasn't been much time yet, for the full story. I only found out my mother was adopted this morning, when I went back and saw my grandfather.'

'You've had an emotionally intense twenty-four hours, haven't you? And looking after everyone else. How are you doing, yourself?'

'Okay,' he said. 'Exhausted,' he added, more truthfully.

She held out her arms, offering a hug, and he accepted it without hesitation. Not so much from need as from want. Because he liked her and respected her and admired the way she simply got in and did whatever needed to be done. Because his attraction to her had become more than a pleasant flirtation. Because whatever else they might one day become – or not – friends hugged each other for support and sharing.

'You've had a pretty intense time, too,' he said, drawing her closer, making the moment last at least a little longer than a quick hug and release. 'And crap news this morning, on top of it.'

She rested her head against his shoulder. 'Yep. It still smarts like hell. I'll get over it, though. Sometime this century.'

He doubted she'd allow herself to grieve her job for long. Not an action-oriented, problem solving woman like her. The acknowledgement that she'd get over it showed she was already thinking beyond the first shock. She'd still have ups and downs, he guessed, but her resilience would win out.

Over her head, he saw Karl glance their way and grin. He released his hold slowly, and stepped back. 'I haven't forgotten that I promised you that drink. I'll try to be back at the pub in time tonight, if you'll be around.'

'I'm not sure what Mum has planned. But I should be able to make my escape after dinner.'

The way she said it made him picture a much younger Angie. 'Even if you have to climb out through the bedroom window?' he teased.

Her laugh drove some of the shadows from her eyes. 'Oh, I may have done that a time or twenty when I was a teenager. But when your parents own the pub, it's the one place you can't sneak in to. Fortunately, Mum's an early to bed type, though, and I'm long past eighteen, so she won't mind if I go out.'

The paramedics were ready to take Delphi to the waiting ambulance. As he and Angie helped to carry the stretcher along the creek bed, his memory replayed the quiet, perfect pleasure of those few moments of body contact, and of the emotional intimacy they'd shared.

Somehow, in twenty-four hours – twenty-four hours packed with intensity and shared experience – she'd become important to him.

And in just a few days, when his grandfather was well enough to travel, he'd be leaving Dungirri, and Angie.

CHAPTER 7

Angie woke from a long nap to find the late afternoon sun angling low through her window, and the on-again, off-again buzzing of some machine in the near distance. It took her half-asleep brain some seconds to place the sound. Her mother's sewing machine. In the spare room.

How many years since she'd heard that sound on Christmas Eve? When she and her brother were children, they'd tried to guess what Mum-made clothes or toys might be under the tree in the morning. But Nancy had stopped making things, years ago.

Angie brushed her bed-hair into some semblance of neatness and shook some packing creases out of the second dress she'd brought with her before she pulled it on.

The door of the spare room was open, but she tapped on it anyway to give her mother time to hide anything secret. Patchwork star blocks in shades and patterns of pink lay in rows on the bed, with a smaller pile of pieces beside her mother at the sewing machine under the window.

Twenty years, at least, since her mother had done any patchwork. And now she was so absorbed she didn't notice Angie for several seconds until she turned to reach for another piece of fabric.

'Oh! You've woken up. Good. I was thinking I'd have to wake you soon for dinner.'

Angie sat on the edge of the bed and picked up one of the star blocks. Perfect seam intersections. Of course. 'What are you making, Mum?'

'A quilt. For the baby. I remembered I had this in the cupboard. I started making this for you before you went off pink.'

At age four. When her little brother Dave had graduated from baby blues to navy and red and a racing green trike. So much more exciting than pink and ribbons.

'It's pretty,' she assured her mother. 'I'm sure Lissa will love it.'

Her mother kept sewing small pieces together as she talked. 'I want to finish it for tomorrow. Dave phoned and he won't be here until late, so I thought perhaps you and I could have dinner at the pub. Deb is doing a buffet tonight, so it will be quick.'

There was a first – her mother volunteering to have a meal at the pub. Even in the rare times there'd been a cook employed other than her, thirty years of pub cooking meant no pleasure in eating there. Six months' break from the daily grind must have given her some distance. Distance, and a sewing project she was clearly enjoying.

'Sounds like a good plan to me. It's good to see you sewing again, Mum.'

'I thought I might make some clothes for the baby. And maybe some things for you?' The question was hesitant and she rushed on, 'That dress you were wearing last night was very pretty on you. I could make you ones like that.'

'I don't need many dresses, Mum. But you could make some lovely things for yourself.' Something more fashionable, attractive and *younger* than the revolving wardrobe of basic stretch pants, sensible skirts and plain shirts. Hmm, she could feel a quest coming on. 'Maybe we could go to Dubbo for a girls' day out and go fabric shopping for you.'

'We could,' Nancy said slowly, considering the idea. But not dismissing it out of hand or coming up with reasons why not. 'When do you have to go back to work?'

Crunch time. It hadn't been hard to avoid telling her when she came home earlier, because her mother had been most concerned about Delphi and there'd been that story to relate. And now that the moment had come to tell her about the redundancy email . . . Angie realised she *wanted* to tell her, wanted her maternal care and sympathy. Maybe she wasn't quite so adult and mature and independent after all.

Her mother put down her sewing and swivelled in her chair to give her full attention as Angie explained.

'Can they *do* that?' Nancy protested when she finished. 'Isn't there some way you can appeal? There are unfair dismissal laws, aren't there?'

'I'm pretty sure it's all legal. Anyway, I'm not

sure I'd want to keep working for them, since they apparently didn't value my work much.' That point hurt the most – that all of the effort and research and long hours she'd invested in her surveys and plans hadn't mattered in their decision.

Her eyes welled and her mother patted her knee and passed her a tissue box. 'What will you do?' she asked.

Angie blew her nose and wiped away the tears, willing them to stay under control. 'I guess I start hunting for another job after Christmas. I've got savings – I was planning to put a deposit on an apartment in February – so I won't go hungry for a while, anyway.'

'You could come back here. Set up your own consulting business. Plenty of people on the land are looking for environmental advice. You're known here and you've always been interested in the agricultural side of it, haven't you?'

The idea had occurred to her. That her mother had noted her interests touched her. That she didn't see consulting as a totally crazy, impractical, financially irresponsible possibility boosted Angie's confidence about the idea.

'I'm not going to make any decisions in a hurry, Mum. I'll think about it. Maybe talk to a few people. It would take a while to build a business and be a big step without much security.' Not that an employment contract with a major consulting company had turned out to be secure.

Her mother switched off her machine and began tidying away her sewing tools. 'You wouldn't be spending anywhere near as much on accommodation if you came back to this district. You could rent a house here for what you pay for your room in Sydney. You wouldn't have to earn as much.'

She could *buy* a house here for a small fraction of the price she'd been planning to pay for an apartment in the city. Although with values here depreciating, not appreciating, it didn't rate highly as a good investment.

Too much to think about, too many options to weigh up, and she didn't have to decide today. But the possibility of coming back to Dungirri didn't seem as impossible now as it had even six months ago.

She linked arms with her mother as they walked the short distance. 'Have you given any more thought to Gil's offer, Mum?'

'I talked with Jeanie about it this morning. And . . . I've decided. I phoned the agent this afternoon.' She took a deep breath in as if she was diving into a pool. 'To accept the offer.'

Angie stopped walking and put her arms around her mother in an unaccustomed hug. 'Good on you, Mum. I know that's a huge decision for you. But I think it's the right one.'

'I hope so. I feel . . . ' She gave a small, self-conscious laugh, ' . . . lighter. But it will take some getting used to.'

Lighter, yes. Angie barely resisted the urge to dance down the street instead of walking. Perhaps the pub had been a millstone around her neck, too.

Someone had spent time decorating the courtyard

this afternoon, and in the twilight it sparkled with hundreds of fairy lights strung through the trees and around the building. Candles flickered in stained-glass holders on every table and already many tables were taken. Not so many families tonight. Mostly young people, and some of the older ones without families, or without small children, anyway. At one table some of the RFS volunteers quenched their thirst and wound down after their hard afternoon.

At a long table on the far side she spotted Owen, with Jeanie and a woman Angie recognised as Bella O'Connell, although she hadn't seen her for close on twenty years. She hadn't been home last year or the year before, when intense investigations for missing girls had brought Bella back to Dungirri, but she'd heard all about it. The man with her must be Alec, the police inspector who'd headed up the second investigation. She'd heard about him, too. Positive comments, even before news filtered through that he'd taken up a senior position on the north coast and Bella had moved there with him.

She steered Nancy over to join them, and by luck rather than effort she took the vacant chair next to Owen. 'I didn't think you'd make it back so early,' she said. 'How is Delphi?'

'We've only just got here. Delphi's good. The fracture should set well. There's a locum arrived from Dubbo for a few days and she will probably discharge her tomorrow.'

'So you won't be needed for any more emergencies?'

'No.' Lines of fatigue shadowed his smile lines. 'I

met Bella and Alec at the hospital. Delphi introduced us.'

'Jeanie had phoned me earlier,' Bella said. 'So it wasn't a total surprise to meet a cousin.' She still had the quiet reserve Angie remembered, yet her smile was cautiously friendly, despite what must be the shock of discovering a new branch of the family. Angie had no doubt it would be okay, that new relationship. Owen had already shown respect and consideration for Delphi, and that would count with Bella. Two intelligent, perceptive people would see the best in each other.

The buffet selection of pastas and salads provided a hearty meal and while they ate conversation flowed around the day's events, family history, and Dungirri news and happenings. Bella filled in what she knew of Delphi's life; raising her much-younger brother, running the property after their father's death in the 1960s. Owen shared more about his family, and the life and legacy of Delphi's daughter.

Nancy excused herself after she finished her meal to go home to her sewing and to wait for Dave, but she told Angie she needn't hurry. 'Jeanie's coming with me. We're going to have a quiet cuppa, the two of us.'

A quiet cuppa and a good long natter after a momentous day for their friend, and a life-changing decision for Nancy. A precious thing, the friendship between her mother and Jeanie, and Angie decided she'd give them at least an hour.

Bella and Alec excused themselves, too, tired after their long drive from the north coast.

Which left only Angie and Owen at the table.

Owen poured the last of the table water into her empty glass. 'I promised you a drink.' His mouth quirked in amusement. 'I meant something other than water. But Alec beat me to the first round. What would you like?'

'An apple juice, please.' She eyed the stack of dishes that Megan, working hard, hadn't yet had time to clear. 'How about I take these plates to the kitchen while you get drinks?'

The evening had been planned to be easy on the staff, so the bistro was already closed, the remains of the buffet cleared away. Her hands full of plates, Angie pushed through the swing doors into the kitchen and took them to the bench, where Gil briskly stacked the dishwasher while Deb cleaned the cooking surfaces to a shine. Liam brought a tray of glasses through from the bar and Megan followed Angie in with another stack of plates.

'We're still planning to close early at nine?' Liam directed the question at Gil, but then glanced at Angie to include her. The owner's daughter, although Nancy had left the day-to-day management, and the profits, to Liam and Deb these past few months.

'Yes, close up,' Angie said. 'Big day tomorrow. But you're only opening for lunch, right?'

Liam nodded. 'Three hours, twelve until three.'

'Good. Then after that you guys should take a few days off. Dave and I can hold the fort.' She looked across to Gil, uncertain if he'd heard from the agent about her mother's decision. Or informed his friends.

'Yeah,' he drawled. 'Take a few days off. But then get those business plans of yours polished up and ready. Mrs Butler's accepted my offer for the pub. So once contracts are exchanged and settled, you'll have me to deal with as senior partner.'

Deb cheered and Liam shouted 'Yes!' and grabbed Megan for a dance around the kitchen. Angie left them to their celebration. She'd make sure the best bottle of champagne made it to the kitchen before she left tonight.

She trailed her fingers over the internal brickwork of the hallway on her way back outside. Old bricks, made and laid over a hundred years ago. Beautiful old timbers in the balustrade of the stairs, carved years before motor vehicles first appeared in Dungirri. Hundreds, thousands of people hosted within these walls, drinking, eating, sleeping, through Dungirri's boom mining and forestry years, and the bust years since.

Her family's custodianship of the hotel was ending after decades. A huge part of her own life. But time to move on, for her mother and herself and her brother. Time for her to move on, too, from her job, and find new work, a new beginning.

'You look thoughtful,' Owen observed as she rejoined him at the table.

The glow from the candle and from the fairy lights in the trees highlighted the features of his face, the strong lines of cheek and jaw, the depth of character in his eyes.

'I was just musing on endings and beginnings. I seem to be in the middle of a few, just now.' And which was Owen? A beginning of something more than friendship between the two of them? Or an ending, because he'd be leaving Dungirri again soon?

She didn't know. She didn't have opportunity to contemplate the questions, because Lexi came over and sat down without waiting for an invitation, elbows on the table and enthusiasm sparkling in her eyes.

'Hey, Angie, you'll be in this, won't you? We're planning the inaugural Dungirri Boxing Day cricket match. Guys versus girls. We reckon we can field at least ten aside.'

The idea appealed, but she barely had time to answer before Karl came, drink in hand, to co-opt Owen for the men's team, and others drifted over, cheerfully debating how many overs should be bowled per innings, and who should be umpires, and how large a bar tab the losing team should provide for the winning team.

By the time Liam came to collect empties and close up, the plan for the match was all sorted, and despite the evaporation of her chance for a quiet drink with Owen, the energy of the idea and the community spirit it represented buoyed her with optimism for Dungirri.

'I believe I promised to walk you home,' Owen said quietly as everyone started to leave.

Angie smiled. There might be a chance for quiet time together after all. 'I haven't had any alcohol. I won't be staggering home and falling over.'

'That's even better. But if Santa runs you down in his sleigh, I can pick you up.'

'Okay. But I just need to go to the bar, first.'

He waited at the door while she went behind the bar, found a bottle of French champagne in the back of the fridge, and paid for it at the register. Liam, putting chairs on tables, saw Owen waiting and gave her a cheeky, knowing grin . . . until she handed the bottle to him.

'For you and Deb and Megan and Gil,' she told him. 'Congratulations on your new business venture. And thank you. For saving the pub.'

Her vision blurred as she left Liam holding the bottle and walked out of the pub with Owen.

He held the gate from the courtyard on to the street open for her. 'I take it your mother has sold the pub?'

'Yes. To Gil Gillespie. It will be in good hands. But it's kind of the end of an era, you know?' The waves of emotion kept coming and she stopped to wipe tears from her eyes before she did trip over. 'Sorry,' she said. 'I'll be right in a minute.'

'It's a significant change for you. It's okay to cry.' He touched a finger to her cheek and brushed a tear away with his thumb. The gentleness of the caress almost made her howl again.

Behind them, the lights in the bar flicked out and her sense of responsibility kicked her emotions into second place. 'You've got your key to the main door, haven't you?'

'Yes. I won't be left wandering the streets all night.'

The light humour helped her equilibrium. 'Good. Otherwise Santa might run *you* down.'

They strolled, side by side, along the row of empty

shop-fronts and for something safe and unemotional to say she told him what each of the shops had been. 'That used to be the bakery. It closed when I was in primary school. This one was the butcher's shop. All local meat, slaughtered and dressed by the butcher himself. This was a newsagent, and this one-' She paused at the window with the murals and the poster for the carol service, where she'd first met him. 'This used to be Doctor Russell's consulting rooms. He retired years ago, and he died recently. We haven't had a doctor here since he retired. And that,' she said honestly, leaning back against the window to look up into his face, 'is my wishful thinking, not a hint.'

Nothing moved in the quiet road, just the two of them in the glow from the street light.

He took a small step closer, one hand on the glass beside her head, the other touching her face. 'I can't stay,' he said. 'Granddad's life is in Brisbane.'

'I know. But I'm glad you came, even if just for a while.'

She drew his head to hers and found his mouth, warm and gentle, their kiss exploring and deepening as they moved close, body to body, passion and desire and pleasure and trust her only awareness.

Until the sweep of headlights and the blast of a car horn dragged her back to reality. The ute turned into her mother's driveway nearby.

Still in Owen's arms, her pulse racing, she gave him a last, brief kiss and said against his mouth, 'That's my little brother. Trust him to interrupt a perfect moment.'

'Little brothers do that,' he murmured, and it was

a long moment before they drew reluctantly apart.

'I'll see you tomorrow,' she promised, and it was the only promise she could make to him because after tomorrow he might be gone.

'Yes.' With one last brush of his lips against hers he left, and she watched him walk down the street for a moment before she went inside to her family.

~

Owen woke in the early light to the sound of a magpie carolling on the veranda outside his room. With his hands behind his head, he lay awake, enjoying the joyful pure sound of the bird greeting the day. A sound of Australia. Of home.

Dungirri. Christmas Day. He no longer believed in doctrine and gospel, but taking time to honour and celebrate teachings of compassion and love, of healing and peace-making and unity? He could do that, with a whole heart.

A whole heart, and a full one. These few days in Dungirri had proved to be an emotional adventure, in a vastly different way to the challenges of his work overseas. A roller-coaster ride, with his grandfather's illness, the revelations about Delphi, and the unexpected strength of his feelings for Angie. A *personal* roller coaster ride, affecting him as an individual.

The realisation came that in these past years of work with MSF he'd been focused on saving lives, on healing people, on fighting for the most basic needs for displaced people and endangered communities . .

. yet despite his passion and commitment to justice, they weren't *his* people or communities. Unlike them, he had the privilege and the ability to be able to leave at any time and return to Australia. Yet he'd neglected his own life, put it on hold, all his energies directed to his work, not to nurturing and sustaining his relationships with his own family, and friends. Not to sustaining his own emotional well-being.

No surprise he'd been feeling burnt-out, on edge, when he'd arrived in Dungirri.

But he owed his grandfather a lifetime of love and inspiration, and he might have only a short time left with him. Everything else – his career, his life, Angie – had to wait.

Wide awake now, he gave up any thought of going back to sleep. He showered and shaved as quietly as he could in the old, shared bathroom. There had been no time for Christmas shopping and he had only the small gift for his grandfather that he'd brought from Baghdad: a slim volume of Iraqi poets, translated into English. But he did have the guitar, and music was perhaps another gift he could give.

He spent fifteen minutes on his laptop, searching for and downloading several pieces of music, old favourites he should be able to remember well enough.

Someone had set out the makings for a simple breakfast in the bistro and he helped himself to coffee and toast before he set off for Birraga. The low angle of the early sun crowned the treetops with gold as he drove, the road quiet with barely any other vehicles.

On the edge of Birraga, he pulled in to a park by the river. With no-one to hear except the birds, he sat at a picnic table with the guitar and practised for almost an hour while the sun rose higher and the gentle morning warmed to bright day.

As his fingers remembered the movements and his brain switched from reading the notes to playing from memory, the music became a meditation and stilled, for a while, the constant thoughts and alertness in his head. When he finished and set aside the instrument, he remained sitting in the quietness as the birds flittered in the trees and a kangaroo and joey edged their way to the river to drink.

This was his life: this place, this moment, along with the people who mattered to him. He carried that calmness and focus with him as he drove the short distance to the hospital.

He paused at the door of his grandfather's room. Delphi O'Connell sat on the hard chair beside him, her denim shirt from yesterday over a hospital gown, her leg in its cast stretched out, her crutches leaning against the bed. The tissue box was on the bed between them.

'There's nothing to forgive,' Delphi said. 'When the sister told me my baby had died, I guessed then what had happened. The girls at the home – we all respected you. You were always kind and I knew you would look after her. And a doctor's daughter would be educated, be comfortable. Better that than forever wondering where she was, who had adopted her.'

Tears rolled down Bernard's cheeks. 'Thank you,'

he managed to say. 'Bless you. You cannot know . . . the gift that is.'

Delphi blew her nose. 'Thank you for the photo albums and your memories of her. They mean a lot to an old woman.' She reached for her crutches. 'Your grandson is here. I'd better go and get ready to leave.'

She pushed herself to her feet and waved away Owen's offer of help as she wrangled the crutches under her arms. But she stopped before she passed him and met his gaze, eye to eye. 'I guess you want to know who your other grandfather was. He was a stockman on our place. A good man. Hardworking and trustworthy. But he rode his motorbike too fast coming back from Birraga with the engagement ring and collected a tree on that bend near Ghost Hill. And that was that.'

She hobbled out the door without waiting to hear his sympathy or his thanks.

Owen set his guitar down and drew the chair she'd vacated closer to the bed. 'Everything okay, Granddad?'

His hands clasped in his lap, he nodded. 'Yes. It is now. Everything is okay. At last.'

Owen studied his face, more peaceful than he had ever seen it, the lines of worry faded and only age marking it now. Thin and pale but peaceful. 'I'm glad,' he said, and took his grandfather's hand in his. 'Merry Christmas, Granddad.'

'Merry Christmas, Owen. In my suitcase you'll find a pocket watch. It still works. It was my grandfather's. It is yours, now. It may not mean much to you since there is no direct ancestry, but I wanted you to have it.'

Owen's throat thickened. 'Of course it means a lot. A grandfather of the heart and a lifetime of memory is a grandfather, no matter the genetics.'

His grandfather gripped his hand painfully tight. 'So is a grandson.'

When he could, Owen cleared his throat. 'I only have a small gift for you.' He gave him the poetry booklet. 'You've always loved literature as well as music. I thought you might find this poetry interesting. And I happened to buy a guitar the other day. If you like, I can play for you for a short while.'

The smile lit his grandfather's face. 'Please.'

Although the chatter and sounds of visitors and staff and patients drifted from the corridor outside, the noise faded for Owen as he settled the guitar on his thigh, and there was only this small room and his grandfather, pale against the white pillows.

'Do you remember this piece?' he asked as he played the opening notes. 'It's a prelude by that ancestor of Dad's, Oliver Caldwell.'

'I remember it.' His grandfather closed his eyes, focusing his whole attention on the music.

Owen played the prelude, then an arrangement of a Bach cello sonata, and the music flowed from his memory into his fingers without stumbling. He followed the sonata with more Bach, one of his grandfather's Christmas favourites, *Jesu Joy of Man's Desiring*.

When he looked up after the last notes, a slight movement in the doorway caught his eye. A few people listened from the corridor. One of the nurses. Lissa, with a baby carry capsule at her feet. Angie. Her gaze meeting his, she nodded at him and she mouthed a word. *Beautiful*, he thought she said.

His grandfather's eyes flicked open, brimming with moisture.

'One more, Granddad.' By the time he finished the last piece he'd chosen, an arrangement of *Amazing Grace*, his own eyes leaked and a tear fell on to his hand. Angie pulled the door closed, leaving him and his grandfather in privacy.

They were both silent. His grandfather lay quietly, his eyes closed, his breathing slow. At rest. Not the final rest, yet, but Owen had the strong sense that the day would not be far away. Already some of his grandfather's spirit seemed to be transforming, focusing elsewhere.

He laid the guitar back in its case, using the time to compose himself again.

'Thank you, Owen,' his grandfather whispered eventually. 'For a most precious gift.'

Owen could find no coherent words to say.

'Do you remember my friend Kathleen?' Bernard continued. 'I loved her. I could not marry her because . . . I was not free. But I pray for the grace of God to be with her again soon.'

He remembered Kathleen, and the laughing, loving friendship between the two of them. A friendship of decades, until her death five years ago. How could he say to his grandfather, *'Don't go?'*

'She was a beautiful soul,' he managed to say.

'She is.' A beatific smiled graced his grandfather's

face. But after a moment his eyes rested on Owen again and in a total shift of focus said, 'You'll be late for lunch.'

And leave him when he was hinting about dying? 'I can stay here, with you.'

As if he read the fear in him, his grandfather patted his hand. 'I'm not going yet. Can we – what do you call it? Skype? With your brother and sister soon? Perhaps tomorrow?'

'Yes. I'll message them to arrange a time.' And to say, *book flights home*. Which brought him to another question. 'Would you like me to arrange patient transport back to Brisbane?'

'Not yet, lad. Not unless you need to be in Brisbane. It's nice here and I have no friends left there for company.'

Outliving friends – one of the disadvantages of reaching ninety. Owen didn't press the suggestion. He had no need to be in Brisbane, either.

His grandfather reached for the poetry book and Owen found and handed him his reading glasses.

'Thank you,' Bernard said. 'Now, go and have lunch. I will read poetry and rest for a while.' He smiled with warmth and understanding. 'And I will be here when you get back.'

He left his grandfather with some reluctance. In a strange way he believed him, that he would not let go yet, that his spirit, although eyeing the stars, still clung to earth. But for now his breathing was easier, and he seemed more peaceful, as if Delphi's assurances enabled him a level of forgiveness for himself. Ninety years, a good life of service and family, and closure before the end. Bernard seemed content with that, and ready for rest.

Endings and beginnings, Angie had said. The end was coming for his grandfather and there was little Owen could do for him, when the time came, other than make it as painless as possible. But perhaps, perhaps, there were beginnings ahead, too, and this quest that had brought him to Dungirri might show him a way forward.

~

The pub and the courtyard buzzed with voices and laughter as Angie parked her mother's car in the space Liam had reserved for her just outside the gate. Chauffeuring Delphi and Lissa from the hospital was her first duty for the morning, after Christmas breakfast with her mother and Dave. They'd all felt the absence of father and husband, missed his cheesy jokes and bonhomie, but with the pub open for Christmas lunch for the first time in years they were all helping out in one way or another – a healthy distraction from sorrow, and a fitting way to end an era.

'Just let me know if you want a lift home early, Delphi. I can take you if Jeanie's busy. You too, Lissa. I doubt Mrs Russell will stay late but if you want a quiet corner to feed the baby I'll find one for you.'

The baby. Megan Angelina, who might take a while to grow into her name. But Lissa called her Meg, so as not to be confused with her honorary aunt.

The delicious scent from the lamb on the spit roast promised a feast as Angie assisted Delphi out of the car and led her and Lissa through the crowd to the shadiest corner of the courtyard, where Megan, off-duty for the day, and Esther Russell had set a small Christmas tree on the table.

Word had spread, and this particular tree was surrounded with gifts for the baby. Not frankincense or gold or myrrh, but a pram, polished up and shining like new; bibs and baby blankets and a plastic bath; toys for the baby and toiletries to pamper her mother.

Lissa cried when Esther Russell, who she'd only spoken to on the phone, enveloped her in a hug and welcomed her. She cried again when she realised the gifts were for little Meg and her. 'I can't believe . . . I've never . . . Everyone is so *kind*. Thank you. Thank you.'

Angie fetched a cushion and a footstool for Delphi, seated near the tree to minimise the risk of people bumping her leg.

'Everything okay?' she asked her.

'Yes.' Delphi nodded towards Lissa and the array of gifts. 'That's good. As it should be. Good on you for helping the girl.'

'I didn't do much,' Angie protested.

Delphi looked her in the eye. 'Believe me, when a girl finds herself alone and scared, kindness and acceptance go a long way.' She gave a rough laugh. 'Same goes for an old woman. But we like to think we're tougher.'

And that might be as close to a confession of

loneliness that Delphi's pride would allow her. But Bella and Alec arrived and Delphi's face softened. Bella showed few signs of the 'gastro' that had laid her up this morning and resulted in Angie fetching her aunt as well as Lissa. That very tender expression in Alec's attention to his partner spelled out what they hadn't publicly announced yet. Delphi's family was apparently expanding even further.

Angie helped lay out salads, plates and cutlery on a long table outside while her mother and Jeanie managed the second table in the bistro, and Dave assisted Liam in the bar. Although many families with small kids were doing Christmas at home or with grandparents, there was still a crowd of eighty booked in for the relatively simple community meal, supported in part by the local Rotary club who donated and managed the spit roast.

She kept an eye out for Owen while she worked. Perhaps he'd stayed at the hospital with his grandfather. Those moments when he'd played for him had been beautiful and moving and yes, intensely emotional between them at the end. Which is why she'd closed the door.

If he didn't show up soon, she'd message him.

People queued up to help themselves to salads and then collected succulent lamb fresh from the spit and Deb's roasted ham and turkey. In the festive atmosphere Angie joked and laughed with everyone as she kept things flowing smoothly at her buffet table, yet a part of her noted, although she didn't say, what a transformation a year made. Two years ago the whole town had been in shock, reeling from tragedy, ghosts of who they'd once been. Last Christmas there were only a few tiny slivers of hope penetrating the darkness, fragile flames that had taken a long while to burn brightly.

Now, despite the lingering effects of the bus accident, the sense of oppression had lifted. People laughed and relaxed and mingled and discussed dreams and ideas and possible strategies to overcome the challenges facing this small town, isolated from main roads.

They all accepted that it wouldn't be easy, but the shared determination to try gave Angie more hope for Dungirri's future than she'd ever had.

When she spotted Owen, he was coming towards her from the bar, carrying two glasses. She met him half-way, in the quiet space between the door from the bar and the door from the bistro where there were few people to crowd them.

He handed her an apple juice. 'You've been working hard and looked thirsty.'

He'd remembered what she liked to drink. It didn't surprise her. 'I am. I wasn't sure if you were coming. Your grandfather . . . ?'

He acknowledged her unasked question with a wistful smile. 'Is okay. I left him reading poetry. But I stayed in Birraga a little while to have a Christmas call with my brother and sister in the US.'

Not just a Christmas call. He didn't need to say the words. She touched her hand to his arm. 'Whatever you need, just ask. I'm here for you. We're here for you. You have friends here and we'll do whatever we can to help. You know that, don't you?'

He nodded, his warm gaze holding hers. 'Yes. I do. And I'm grateful and glad we came here. I thought when we drove in here that it was in the middle of nowhere, but it turns out that it's a place where he's found a peace he's craved for a long time. And I've found . . .' He looked down at the glass in his hand and he took a moment before he lifted his eyes again to hers. 'I've found a kind of peace, too. And possibilities. For beginnings. I'm not sure where they'll lead, but I find I'm not in a hurry to leave.'

Endings and beginnings. Death and life. Heartbreak and hope. Christmas and the end of the year, a new year on the horizon.

Behind her the courtyard was filled with friends and people she'd known for years, celebrating survival and looking to the future with courage.

She touched her hand to Owen's and hoped he saw the courage and optimism she'd found within herself. 'I find I'm not in a hurry to leave, either. There are definitely possibilities to explore.'

She doubted she'd ever get tired of the way his smile bloomed, the promise it held. She'd kissed him last night and if there weren't eighty people in close proximity now, she'd have stepped straight into his arms and kissed him again. Instead she raised her glass to her lips, took a sip, holding his gaze. He could play the game, too, and did, taking a mouthful from his glass, watching her with a grin.

'What I am in a hurry for,' she said, with a deliberately teasing pause before she finished, 'Is lunch. Let's go and find food, and a table with friends.'

'A great plan,' he agreed.

He stayed by her side as they heaped food on their plates, and they found chairs next to each other at the large table with Delphi and Jeanie and Nancy, Bella and Alec and Kris and Gil, Megan and Lissa and the baby. Generations of Dungirri people. Friends.

Angie's heart felt full of gratitude. And maybe sometime she'd be able to convince people not to refer to this place as the middle of nowhere. The rich diversity of the environment – the Dungirri Scrub, the rivers and creeks that wound through it and across the pasture lands – and its social history of success and struggle, sorrow and joy, made it somewhere unique.

Her somewhere, and she was grateful she'd found her home again. A good beginning for the next chapter of her life.

ACKNOWLEDGEMENTS

I am grateful to so many people who have supported and encouraged me in writing this novella.

Kylie Short generously provided information and advice about SES community first responders, their equipment and procedures.

Dr David Healey and Annette Healey provided advice about medical matters and procedures.

Beattie Alvarez, Kate Thomas and Anna Thomson have been wonderful editors and cheerleaders.

I am especially grateful to Lauren Sadow, whose skills in graphic and print design have made this book possible within the tight timeframes, and who has cheered me on, every step of the way.

Dr Jeremy Fisher and Dr Elizabeth Hale, my PhD supervisors, have kept me on track and encouraged my progress, enabling this work to be part of the creative practice component of my research.

And Gordon has been beside me all these months, always patient, always encouraging.